Eye Lake

Tristan Hughes was born in Atikokan, Canada and brought up around Llangoed, Ynys Mon where he currently lives. *Eye Lake* is his fourth novel.

TRISTAN HUGHES

Eye Lake

PICADOR

First published 2011 in paperback by Picador

This edition published 2012 by Picador
an imprint of Pan Macmillan, a division of Macmillan Publishers Limited
Pan Macmillan, 20 New Wharf Road, London N1 9RR
Basingstoke and Oxford
Associated companies throughout the world
www.panmacmillan.com

ISBN 978-0-330-45198-7

9 8 7 6 5 4 3 2 1

A CIP catalogue record for this book is available from
the British Library.

Typeset by SetSystems Ltd, Saffron Walden, Essex
Printed and bound by CPI Group (UK) Ltd, Croydon, CR0 4YY

Visit **www.picador.com** to read more about all our books
and to buy them. You will also find features, author interviews and
news of any author events, and you can sign up for e-newsletters
so that you're always first to hear about our new releases.

To Tess and Magnus

'*A lake is the landscape's most beautiful and expressive feature. It is Earth's eye . . .*'

The Phantom Shad

I was casting out from the eastern shore of Eye Lake, opposite the second island, when I snagged the top of my grandfather Clarence's castle. Of course I didn't know it was his castle at first; I just thought it was a log or a dead-head or something; but because it wasn't far out from shore and it wasn't that deep – just an inch or two beneath the surface – I decided I'd swim out and fetch my lure. I didn't want to lose that lure. It wasn't much good at catching anything, but it looked great and had come in a box with its own name on it: the Phantom Shad. And that's what it looked like too: a spook minnow, as almost-see-through white as a ghost, with two little red eyes. A bit like my best friend George McKenzie used to look when he was a kid. I'd found it in its box by the edge of Franklin's Trail after some fishermen from Minnesota had gone through (it's worth watching them on the trails because they drop stuff all the time and don't seem to care if they lose it anyhow). You can always tell Minnesotans up here in northern Ontario: they've got bigger beards and newer fishing stuff than anyone else.

Now it may not sound like such a big decision – to

swim for the phantom shad – but it sort of was. I hate swimming in Eye Lake. Its water is brown, the colour of stewed tea, and full of weeds and slime and hundreds and hundreds of drowned trees. In the shallow bays some of them stick up out of the water, and in the deeper parts they just lurk there below the surface. (The Sunken Forest, that's what my uncle Virgil used to call it: the forest they sank when they dammed and detoured the Crooked River to get at the iron ore. Some people call the whole place the floodwaters.) But anyway, what with all the weeds and slime and trees it's not somewhere you'd want to dip your toe in even. I've caught slubes – which is what we call pike up here in Crooked River – as big as your leg in it. Hungry slubes, who wouldn't be that fussy about eating the odd toe or two.

So it was a tough decision but in the end I went in, holding my line in my hand, trying not to look beneath me and trying not to imagine getting my legs and arms all tangled up in the weeds and underwater branches. Only when I got to the shad I found it wasn't snagged on any log or drowned tree or underwater branches – it was snagged on the ridge of a roof! An inch below the surface were the slimy, waterlogged boards of a roof! That really freaked me, realizing what it was, and then forcing myself to look closer and make sure it wasn't just a boat turned upside down or something. But it wasn't. It was the roof of a building, a thin square building like a tower. Through the brown water I could see where it fitted onto log walls, and as I kicked about with my feet trying to tread water one of them bumped against the logs and slipped into a hole that I knew then was a window. There was no doubt. It was Clarence's castle and I'd found it.

I guess I always knew it was down there in the lake somewhere, in a way, in the way you hear about something so many times you kind of know it must be there, somewhere. Like the *Titanic*. Or Atlantis. Or Bad Vermillion. But they're never things you ever expect to actually find, let alone hook. I might as well have snagged a unicorn, or one of those sea monster things in Virgil's book of old maps. Krakens. That was one of his jokes when he'd cast somewhere he thought there were big fish: 'There be Krakens,' he'd say. When I snagged the bottom he'd say (putting on a snooty English voice, like the Earl's), 'I do believe, young Eli, that you've caught Canada.' And I do believe, old Virgil – I said to him in my head – that I've caught Clarence's . . . and then I shut up because I realized then that Virgil must have known exactly where it was all along because he never fished near this shore, not once, not ever. It was no joking matter.

I saw a show once on the history channel about the *Titanic*. There was all that sad stuff about the guys playing on their violins as it went down and them not having enough boats for everyone, but the bit that really stuck in my head was that it hit an iceberg because icebergs can be small above the water and big below it. Ninety per cent of their mass, the presenter said . . . or something like that. A lot bigger. And as I floated about in the brown water I knew there must be a whole bunch more of Clarence's castle below me, not just the tower part that I'd hooked.

I'd seen a picture of it: a photo that my Nana kept

hidden down in the basement of number one O'Callaghan Street, along with the rest of Clarence's stuff. She didn't like it much, I reckon, but she kept it anyway and so I saw it. The castle was made out of red pine logs. It was a big barn-shaped building, about thirty feet high, with a tower at one end about forty-something high. Now I don't know if that's what a proper castle looks like, but it sure didn't look like a cabin; it didn't look like nothing built around here. And anyway, that's what the old-timers called it: a castle, Clarence's castle. In the photo he's standing in front of it on a wide lawn – if you looked real close you could see flowers coming up through the grass – wearing an old suit full of rips and tears. To be honest he doesn't look that over the moon about finishing his castle. There's a sad, pinched frown on his face and he seems to be staring off to the side of the photo, as if he's expecting something, or someone, to arrive from that direction. And that's pretty much the last photo that ever got took of him.

I was thinking about all of this – and a lot of other things too – while I was out there in the water. Like who I was going to tell about what I'd found and how I wished I could've told Nana or Dad or Virgil; how they would've acted all excited and impressed the same as when I'd catch something when I was a kid and they'd make a fuss of me as though I'd brought home a pot of gold from the end of a rainbow, even if it was only a slube, and how that'd make me feel about ten feet tall. I wished I could've told them – that they were still around to tell. And then I was thinking about why I'd found it now, after all this time, and not before. But it wasn't such a miracle, I reckoned. The waters of Eye Lake were falling; I'd been noticing that the past few days – in some places the waterline was almost a foot or two below where it usually was this time of year. I wasn't exactly sure where the water was going but I had my suspicions. In my experience most water is like a good dog: give it time and it'll find its way home, back where it belongs. Not like Clarence, who never came home, who never came back, even though now his castle was slowly clawing its way towards the daylight again.

But then I got to thinking about that scene in *Jaws* where the man's swimming beside a sunken ship, and he comes to a hole in its side and a giant eel tries to bite him and then a head falls out of the hole. And I got to thinking as well about how some folks said it was called Eye Lake because all the people who'd ever drowned in it looked up from its bed with open eyes – Virgil called them 'the watchers'. I wasn't too happy about being in the water any more then. Not at all. So I grabbed the phantom shad and swam back to the shore.

Afterwards I walked back down Franklin's Trail to the Poplars. I'd been living there for two years, in the Tamarack dorm. There were Pine and Birch and Poplar dorms too but Buddy Bryce, who owns the place, said I could pick whatever one I wanted to stay in and I liked the name Tamarack best, even though strictly treewise I'd probably go for the Poplar or Birch. 'Take your pick, Eli,' he said. 'We'll not be getting visitors any time soon.'

Last year Buddy told me I should put a sign on the entrance to my dorm, below the Tamarack one, saying 'Caretaker'. 'Kinda make things more official,' he said. And by things he meant me looking after the place, which is what I did, for a hundred and fifty bucks a month and a place to stay because number one O'Callaghan Street wasn't fit for living in. That's what Buddy told me when he first offered me the job. 'Your place isn't fit for living in any more, Eli,' is what he said, looking at it kind of disgusted from over the fence where he lives, at number two O'Callaghan Street. He'd been looking at it like that for a few years, as if he'd made everything about his place pretty much perfect – like his garden and his painted fence and his new hot tub – apart from this one thing. 'Look,' he said, 'I got an idea that'd maybe help you out a bit.' Buddy's the kind of wily old-timer who makes out he's doing you a favour when really he's getting something he wants, which in this case was my house pulled down and put out of his sight. But I never did pull it down, which was lucky I guess – especially for an O'Callaghan. My family wasn't ever considered big on luck.

On the beach in front of the Hematite Conference Room (there's a Granite one too, on the other side of the site) Sarah Anderson was taking a walk with her kid, Bobby. He was covered in sheets like a mummy to keep the blackflies off him because he had what she called 'delicate skin'. And to be honest I knew how he felt: it was the first week in June and the blackflies were just starting to get real bad – we'd all have delicate skins until we'd been bitten good enough to get used to it. Sometimes you'd even see the moose going nuts with them, running crazy and lankily through the bush to keep them off.

'Hey there, Eli,' she called, waving at me.

I waved back and then sort of just dawdled about, wondering if she meant for me to come over and talk. She strolled over to me then.

'Jesus, these flies,' she said. 'They're abominable.' I had to think about that for a minute and then it came to me.

'Like the snowman,' I said.

'What?' she said, looking at me confused.

'Abominable,' I said, 'like the snowman.' The truth was I wasn't so sure what it meant.

'Yes, of course, like the snowman,' she laughed, as if I'd made a joke and was a real comedian. I felt a bit nervous after that, thinking I'd have to tell another joke to keep things up. Luckily at that moment Bobby came up beside her.

'Hullu E-lu,' he said from under the sheet that was wrapped around his face. There was a swarm of bugs around his head, like there is around Pigpen's head in those Snoopy cartoons. Blackflies aren't so dumb: they can smell a delicate skin a mile off.

'Hey there,' I said. 'These bugs getting you good, eh?'

Bobby was a nice kid and I felt kind of more comfortable talking to him than Sarah, even though she was nice too.

'What you get?' Bobby asked – I was still holding my fishing rod, I realized – pulling the sheet off his mouth. Some of the flies flew right in there when he opened it, and he started coughing.

'No luck,' I told him.

'Nothing?'

'Not a bite.' And suddenly I really wanted to tell him about the castle – to pull it out like a magician's coin from behind his ear so he and Sarah would be impressed. I could feel it pushing up on my tongue just like the castle itself was pushing up against the surface of the lake, wanting to get out of there. But I managed to bite on it. It was like I was hiding a piece of treasure or something and didn't know quite what to do with it yet.

A bush plane went buzzing over us and it seemed funny to me how even the human stuff round here was beginning to be like bugs. I was going to try making a joke about it but could see that getting complicated, so I didn't. And besides, Sarah was staring up at the plane with a strange look on her face – not exactly sad, but not happy either. It was one of Buddy's planes and that meant Billy was flying it.

I didn't know how things stood between her and Billy. They'd been on and off for years. The first time they were on they lived together next door to me at Buddy's, who's Billy's dad. They'd sit out in the garden a lot and sometimes I'd go over there for a few beers. But then she went off to Alberta for a couple of months and when she came back she was pregnant; apparently she'd been pregnant before she left only it didn't show till she came back. I didn't see much of them then. She kept herself inside mainly and Billy was out flying his planes most days and Buddy started cutting the grass all the time as if it was growing ten feet every day. He painted the fence three times that summer.

When Bobby was born that made him the fourth 'B'.

It was a big joke among the Bryces, that they were all 'B': Brenda the mum and Buddy and Billy. They called themselves the Three Bs. It's what they named Buddy's tackle and bait store – 3B's Live Bait and Tackle – as well as his fly-in outfitters' business – 3B's Outposts. Buddy owned a bunch of things. He'd sort of started collecting them after the mine closed down, as if he needed something to put his energy into, all the energy he'd put into the mine before. Buddy always liked to be doing stuff.

They never changed the name to 4B's though. The next summer I'd sometimes see little Bobby out in his pushchair in the garden and catch Buddy looking at him a bit like he did my house. And then he'd look away and start pruning his apple trees or weeding the flower beds. When Sarah went to Alberta the second time – about three years later – none of the Bs seemed that upset. I thought she'd be gone for good then but I guess things didn't work out because two years later she was back – in the Bryces' house for a while and then out at the Poplars, in the Pine dorm. I'd already been out there on my own for a year and was happy enough to get some neighbours. Just the two of them, mind you – Billy stayed put at O'Callaghan Street and only came out for 'visits'. The funny thing was it was Buddy who ended up visiting more often. He'd stopped looking at Bobby like he did my house and kept pretending he needed to talk to me about things at the Poplars when really I knew he was just coming to see Bobby.

'What were you using?' Bobby asked me. I knew he was hoping it was minnows because when I did I'd always keep a few spare for him to play with. I was just the same at his age. I used to fish for them too, with a bent pin and a piece of bacon fat, and I remembered how I was going to show him how to do that. He was about seven and young enough to get plenty excited about it.

'A crank bait,' I told him.

'What's that?'

I took the phantom shad out of my pocket and showed it to him.

'Can I hold it?'

I gave him the box and he turned it around in his hands. The front of it was see-through and he peered right into its red eyes. He looked pretty damn happy with it and I thought what the hell, I almost lost it today anyways.

'You have it,' I told him.

'Really?'

'Really.'

Except then I noticed Sarah staring straight at me as if she were trying to talk to me with her eyes. Her lips were all puckered together.

'But I'm sure Eli doesn't want to give away his special lure, Bobby,' she said. 'He's only trying to be nice – but that's a special lure and you shouldn't take it from him.' She was using that voice that's really two voices at once, one soothing and friendly for the kid, the other hissed and pissed for you, as if your ears are meant to pick up an extra frequency when you're older that kids can't hear, like a bat.

Bobby and I stood there confused. He wanted the lure a lot and I wanted him to have it.

'You better give it back then,' Sarah said. Bobby passed

it back to me as if he was passing back a big lump of gold. His eyes were wetting up and he didn't want me to see so he turned away and sulked towards the beach with his cloud of bugs swarming around his head.

'Really, Eli,' Sarah said. 'I don't want him playing around with hooks, not without supervision – not without someone to show him.' She sounded mad.

'I'm sorry,' I said. 'I didn't think.'

'No,' she said. 'You didn't. Nobody thinks.'

And then she started crying.

I couldn't understand why it was such a big deal, but I decided I'd better start teaching Bobby about hooks and stuff as soon as I could.

The Tamarack dorm has twelve rooms – six facing the lake, six facing the woods – and I've stayed in every one of them. Sometimes I've stayed in a different room every night of the week as if I was on holiday and staying in different hotels along the way, the same as when me and Dad drove to Toronto once. And I could've stayed in all the other rooms in all the other dorms if I'd wanted to because Buddy was right: nobody was going to visit the Poplars any time soon.

It'd seemed a good plan when they'd built it. A wilderness conference centre is what they called it; somewhere for business people to come and talk and get a good wholesome taste of bush living. Except they didn't much enjoy the taste of bush living in the winter – so that was seven months out of the year gone – and they didn't much like the taste of the bugs either – so that was at least another three months gone. And two months a year isn't going to keep any place open. Buddy bought it for nothing and whatever plans he had for it I didn't know them, just that he wanted the buildings looking after. Maybe he was thinking of a fishing camp, but now the waters of the lake were falling that wasn't going to be such a great plan. We hadn't had much luck with things in Crooked River the last thirty years or so.

Mostly when I moved rooms I picked the ones facing the woods. There was something about having the lake outside the window – especially at night – that did for me. The sound of the loons calling across the water and the cry of the trains from far away and the way you'd sometimes be able to see the trees in the bays, sticking up out of the surface in the moonlight like thin bony fingers – all that'd start me thinking and then I knew I'd not be sleeping any time soon. So maybe it was a bit stupid that I picked one of those rooms to lie down in after meeting Sarah and Bobby.

I don't know how long I lay there but I was drifting off and eventually it must have got dark because when I woke up I couldn't see anything except a star or two reflected off the lake. And I was glad that I couldn't see much because I'd already seen plenty in my sleep. In it I was as young as Bobby and the phantom shad had hooked me through the hand and dragged me down into the lake, and into the sunken forest. When I hit bottom I started walking along these underwater trails, beneath the trees, with the weeds hanging off their branches like leaves and swaying about in the water as if it was wind. The shad was sort of leading me along on its hooks and I could see its eyes looking at me, except that they'd multiplied and turned into the eyes of the watchers – white and bloodshot and staring. And one of them was George McKenzie and another one was Clarence. Then I came to the castle and the weeds were hanging off its walls too, like ivy on old houses, and the windows were as dark as drop-offs on the edges of reefs. When the door began to open I tried to step backwards but I couldn't and when it'd opened all the way there were George and Clarence staring at me and beckoning me in. I looked up but there was no sign of the surface and in the window of the tower I saw my dad rocking back and forth on a chair with his head in his hands and little bubbles coming out of his mouth. I kept trying to turn around and go back but the shad kept pulling me towards the door. And then there was a knocking sound and it sounded so loud I thought my head would explode with it, but as I woke up I realized it was only a normal knocking sound coming from my door.

When I opened it I found Sarah there, standing in the night, slapping her ears and neck to keep the bugs off. Her hair was so black it was like her face was just floating there in the darkness.

'Can I come in?' she asked.

'Sure,' I said.

We stood inside behind the closed door and she kept looking down at the floor and then up at me.

'Look Eli, I just wanted to say I'm sorry about before. I didn't mean to snap at you like that.'

'It's nothing,' I said.

'No,' she said, 'it's not nothing. I don't know what's got into me recently.'

'But you were right,' I said.

'About what?'

'About that lure.'

'What about it?' she asked, as if she'd forgotten it already. I wished I could.

'About Bobby not having it,' I said. 'You know, it's not so special – I reckon I'm going to throw it away anyhow. Bobby shouldn't have it. It's better to start out with a bent pin or something . . .'

'I don't care about the frigging lure, Eli . . . I'm sorry, I'm sorry . . . I don't know what's wrong with me.'

And then she was crying again. I didn't know what to do.

'Do you want a glass of milk?' I asked.

She was crying for quite a long time, sitting at the table in the kitchen, sobbing and then trying to talk and then sobbing again. I couldn't figure out what she was saying exactly but mostly it was about how she wasn't this kind of person. She said that a lot. I'm not this kind of person, Eli. I hate being like this. Sometimes when she was sobbing she'd put her face in her hands like my dad in the tower and you could see the fly bites on her neck, all red and sore-looking like her face.

When I gave her the glass of milk she stared at it as if it were the nectar of the gods. That's what Virgil used to say when he had a beer sometimes: 'Ah, the nectar of the gods.' And then she looked at me in a funny kind of way and said: 'You're one of the few really decent people I know, Eli. Do you know that?' I didn't.

When she got up to go she thanked me for listening and being so helpful and understanding. But I'd hardly said anything. And I'd hardly understood anything neither. Most people in Crooked River thought I didn't understand much of anything except for fishing.

After she was gone I went and put the phantom shad straight in the garbage and sat down at the table trying not to think of anything at all, except how I wished I had a TV out here because I knew I wasn't going to be sleeping much.

Happy 100th, Crooked River

The next morning I decided to walk into Crooked River and have a talk with Mr Haney and Gracie McKenzie over at the museum. It was only a few miles from the Poplars into town – down an old dirt road – but I took my time about it, dawdling my way along in the sunshine. The warmth felt good on my skin and the clearness of the sky was a big relief to me after the night before. There was a sweet smell drifting out of the woods from the wild strawberry plants coming through, and the leaves were all coming out too. There's a sadness about the woods in the winter, all naked and spindly and see-through in the snow except for the pines and spruces, a sorrowful black-and-whiteness like the X-ray of a sick person. And then suddenly it's gone. Everything here gets going fast – the bugs and animals come rushing out, the plants and leaves push through in a hurry, the whole bunch of them trying to cram their living into the short summer. There's a hum and buzz in the June air, as if a million invisible little speeded-up machines were working away in it.

When I got to the outskirts I saw they'd put a placard up beside the town sign. *Happy 100th*, it said. The sign itself said *Crooked River: Population 2851*. They hadn't got around to changing it for a couple of years now. Maybe they were hoping things would pick up a bit first.

Happy 100th. I'd forgotten it was the town's birthday. As I walked past I noticed the placard had already started curling up at the edges.

On Main Street, Billy pulled up beside me in his new truck. Its front wheel sank into a big pothole like a partridge fluffing itself down in the dirt. There were a bunch more holes in the street this year and the other cars and trucks were weaving their way around them as if their drivers were drunk. It was a good thing Main was wide enough for about ten cars and trucks to weave down it at once – even though there were never more than one or two, and quite often none at all. Sometimes it looked like those roads in westerns, the ones with tumbleweed rolling across them.

'Hey there Eli,' Billy said, leaning out the window. 'How's she going?'

'Fine,' I said.

'Whatcha been up to out there in the boonies?' With his new moustache it was hard to work out the look on his face.

'Not much,' I said. 'Some fishing.'

'Just some, eh,' he said. There was a sort of winking in the way Billy spoke to me; there always had been, as if I needed special signals to help me catch up with him. 'Don't you worry, I'm not going to tell Buddy what you get up to out there.'

I'd known Billy since we were both kids, since we were

both babies. I was Population 5671 and Billy was Population 5670. He beat me by two days, which made Buddy happy – to have a Bryce get somewhere first. They used to make a big fuss back then about the first baby born in the year (they don't bother with it now) and Buddy still had the photo of Billy in the hospital – cut out from the *Crooked River Progress* – on the wall of his house. *No. 1. 1972*, said the caption beneath it. In my house we never made such a big deal about me having got born.

To tell the truth I don't think I even liked Billy that much when we were babies, if babies can be picky like that. But what can you do? You don't get any choice who you get born near and grow up with, not in a town like Crooked River where there's a whole lot of miles of nothing on either side of you. And after that amount of time knowing someone, you're pretty much something for ever – even if that something isn't exactly friends.

'So . . .' he said with a little nod, pushing himself up in his seat some. He was kind of short, and wiry too – like his dad.

I said nothing.

'Just fishing, eh.' He sounded the same way he used to sound when he got worried I was playing with his toys.

I said nothing.

'Well, I'll be seeing you about then, Eli,' Billy said, revving his engine and pulling out of the pothole.

'Hey,' he called back to me. 'You should sign up for the 3B's Bass Classic this year.'

But before I could answer he was already careering his

way down the street, between the potholes, kicking up a cloud of reddish dust behind him.

'So what do you think then, Eli?' Mr Haney asked me. He was standing outside the museum with his hands on his hips, admiring a new poster above the entrance. *CENTENNIAL*, it said. *1901–2001*. It looked like I was pretty much the only person in town who'd forgotten it was its birthday. 'Come in, come in. I think you'll like what we've done inside.'

Inside the kids from the school had drawn a bunch of pictures on the wall. Up above them they'd written in big letters, *Crooked River: The Little Town Who Could*.

One of the pictures was of Clarence, looking strange in crayon and standing beside the blue squiggle of the Crooked River. There was a canoe pulled up behind him on the bank and he was holding a paddle in his hand. 'The arrival of the town's first white settler,' the children had written below him. He was in another picture too, holding a hand saw and standing beside his hotel on O'Callaghan Street. *The Pioneer Hotel – Our First Building*. Further on there was a young Buddy driving into town in front of a boxcar loaded with iron ore. *The First Iron Ore From Red Rock Mine*. For some reason there was a pine tree sticking up out of it.

'Welcome to the new art gallery, Eli,' Gracie croaked, not sounding quite as impressed with it as Mr Haney. She was sitting in her glass-walled office smoking a cigarette. You weren't supposed to smoke in the museum but these days nobody told Gracie what to do, and even if they did she wouldn't pay no mind to them. She looked a lot older than she was; she'd started looking older than she was ever since George went missing. In between puffs she sometimes took a gulp of oxygen from a mask attached to a canister beneath her desk. 'Who knows, maybe we'll get a set of swings and some playdough for our next exhibit.'

'It's been great to have the whole community involved in our celebrations,' Mr Haney said to me, looking sideways in Gracie's direction. Mr Haney used the word community a lot when he spoke.

'Jesus, Tom. I'd thought you'd finished up with the speeches yesterday.'

'I was just telling Eli how gratifying it is to have the community all pitch in . . .'

Gracie stubbed her cigarette into a white bowl and looked out the window. She'd been working at the museum since I was a kid. Mr Haney was a bit of a newcomer: he'd only been there ten years.

What I'd wanted to do was tell them about finding Clarence's castle – it seemed like something the museum should know – but now I wasn't so sure. From where I stood it seemed like the museum had it all figured out about Clarence already: the first this and the first that: Crooked River Population 1. The kids had given him wide crayon smiles as if he was just as happy as could be, as if putting Crooked River onto a map was what he'd wanted to do the whole time. It looked like he was really looking forward to the birthday party and blowing out the hundred candles.

But it hadn't all been like that. His face in the photo didn't look like that at all. And when I thought of it my circle of tempers – which is what Dr Gashinski used to call it – began to spin and I forgot how good the sun had felt and everything started to feel as black and white as the photo, as sorrowfully black and white as winter.

'So to what do we owe the pleasure?' Mr Haney called down to me. He was standing on a chair tying some balloons up over the door.

'Of what?' I asked.

'Of your *company*, Eli.'

'Oh,' I said. 'I just wanted to see . . .' I glanced around for something I might have come to see, even though I'd already seen pretty much everything in the museum before. There was an iron drill in one corner and a board covered in old front pages from the *Crooked River Progress*. In another there was a bunch of rusty-looking knives, a wood stove, and a cupboard full of tin pots and pans. *An Old-Timer's Kitchen*, the sign beside it said. The stove had sat for years in our basement in O'Callaghan Street before Nana gave it to the museum; it seemed like if something sat for long enough in a basement in Crooked River then it'd become something historical and find its way here.

I took so long about deciding that Mr Haney must've thought I needed helping out.

'Ah, the murals,' he said. 'You came to see the murals.'

I looked at Mr Haney for another second or two.

'The paintings,' he said. 'The paintings on the wall.'

How stupid, I thought. I should've picked them right from the start.

'Yes,' I said.

'There's some of your grandfather, you know.'

'I reckon he's probably figured that out, Tom,' Gracie piped up. 'So how's life treating you out at the Poplars then, Eli?'

Gracie had always kept an eye out for me because George and me used to be best friends.

'Pretty good,' I said, even though at that moment nothing felt that good. I wished I could just talk to Gracie on her own and tell her about the castle. She knew about it. She'd known Dad and Nana and Virgil and I'm sure they'd talked about it. Having something to tell about and nobody to tell it to suddenly seemed a terrible thing. And I had a lot to tell Gracie, even besides the castle. I knew that.

'Maybe you'd like to help with these balloons,' Mr Haney said. He was wobbling on the chair. Every winter he got a bit fatter – the opposite of the animals, who came out in the spring scrawny and thin.

'Jesus, Tom. Eli doesn't want to be messing about in here. If you want to turn this place into a kindergarten you can do it on your own.'

Normally I would've been happy to help but right then I didn't want to do anything except go home. To my old home. Number one O'Callaghan Street.

Back outside, Main Street was its wide and empty self: in Crooked River, it's not just the tarmac that has holes in it. There are holes in the line of storefronts that run along it too. Some of them are just fronts anyway: tall rectangles of board that've been there for years where nobody's bothered to pull them down or put closed signs on. *Gil's Radio Electric. O'Brian Services. Bob Moffatt Supply Ltd.* I've forgotten what some them used to sell. In other places there's nothing at all, only empty lots overgrown with weeds and brush, and here and there beside them a store with a new lick of paint and extra-special deals advertised in the window, as if they're scared of going the same way. Sometimes I think the street looks kind of like a hillbilly's grin: trying to be welcoming but with some of its teeth rotting and others missing altogether. And behind, the pale green gums of the woods.

Maybe Buddy's right about it. Maybe number one O'Callaghan Street isn't fit for living in any more. But I still like visiting it. If you don't regard it too close – at where the paint is peeling off and the windowsills are sagging and stuff like that – it looks almost the same as it's always looked. The fence still goes around the big garden, with the crab apple tree in the middle and the pile of rotting boards that used to be Clarence's hotel on the far side. The porch still sits facing into the garden and the chimney from the wood stoves in the basement and living room still pokes out of the roof, tilting to the side the same as it has for a good few years now.

Winter had been hard on the place this year and the porch was falling through pretty badly. Some of the floorboards were so rotten my foot went right through when I stepped inside the door. I pulled it out and went to lie down on the old settee. It was getting on the mouldy side and there was fluff coming out where a squirrel or something had got in and started chewing on it. They'd probably be asking to have it in the museum before long.

When I was a kid Nana would let me sleep on the porch settee sometimes. I loved lying there and just listening. You could hear the frogs and the crickets and occasionally Jake Ottertale or Jim Clement muttering to themselves as they zigzagged down the sidewalk to the Red Rock Inn. And sometimes Jim would stop over for a drink or two with Virgil, and they'd sit on the porch talking while I lay there listening.

But my favourite thing was the sounds of the trains. You could hear some of them being shunted on the tracks at the end of the road near the roundhouse, creaking and groaning like stiff old men getting out of their chairs. But best of all were the ones that went straight through. You'd hear them a-ways out to begin with, their horns making an echoey lonely loon-cry in the dark, and then you'd start to feel them coming too: a low, distant rumbling, like a tremor, gently shuddering and juddering the windows, getting slowly bigger and bigger, until the settee and the pictures on the walls and the whole frame of the porch were quaking and the whole night was clanging and whooshing and banging. And then it'd be past. The sound and the shaking would shuffle back into the dark and I'd lie there feeling like I'd been tucked in. The next night there'd be another train and knowing that made me feel happy and safe and ready to go to sleep.

But hardly any trains came through these days and right

now I couldn't sleep, even though I'd not slept the night before. Whenever I closed my eyes the shape of the castle would be there and their faces – George's and Clarence's and Dad's – would be watching me from the windows and doors with big bubbles coming out their mouths, like the bubbles people speak through in cartoons, like they were full of talk that you'd only be able to hear when they got to the surface and popped. So I stopped trying to close my eyes and went through into the living room.

On one side of the room Virgil's books still sit on the tall, wide shelf he'd built for them. They cover nearly the whole wall. I'm not so sure where he got all of them but a lot came through the post. Every month he'd come back from the post office with a package under one arm and a bottle of whiskey under the other, settle himself down on the cane chair beside the wood stove in the kitchen, and announce to the room, 'Speak to me now if you have to or forever hold your peace, 'cause for the next few hours I'm only listening to the muses.' Then he'd open the package and start reading. Reading, fishing and hunting – that's what Virgil did and that's what he'd always done, ever since he was a kid. In the fall he'd do some hunt guiding for southerners and Americans, in the spring and summer he'd take them out fishing, and in the winter he ran a few trap lines on the north shore of Eye Lake. That's how he made his money, which was never much but always enough.

On the other side of the room, beneath Nana's Helsinki picture, there's a box full of records that've been sitting there for as long as I can remember, and I sat down on the floor beside it and started picking through them.

Virgil used to tell me that the smartest thing you could do was not look behind you, not ever. 'What's gone, well that's gone, Eli, and there's nothing to be done about it, not a damn thing!' Or sometimes, when he took me fishing, he'd say: 'Worry about the ones you get in the boat, not the ones that get away.' Virgil used fishing to explain a lot of things, like keepers and limits and getting your hook set, stuff like that. It was his way of thinking and I kind of believed it too. It was the same as a story we'd learnt in school, about Lot and his wife. In Virgil's mind, to peek over your shoulder was a sure-fire way of turning everything to salt and leaving an awful bitterness on your tongue; that glimpse you felt you couldn't help taking, the one when you'd just about made it – well, that'd be the one that spoilt everything. Move on, is what people say these days. You got to look forwards.

Virgil's theory seemed to cover just about everything – except music. He and my dad used to share the box of records, and leafing through them now I remembered that as far as I could tell every one of them was about losing things and looking back: women were always gone; homes were always lost; and every road the singers travelled was speeding away through the rear window. And sure enough, as if to prove his theory, the times he listened to these records were some of the few times I ever saw my uncle look truly unhappy; sometimes I'd even catch him with the tiniest of tears in his eye, as small as the weeping robin's in his favourite song. But he was still a lot different to his brother – my dad – who always looked like he was listening to those records, even when he wasn't.

Dad was pretty much Virgil's opposite: if there was any way he could crane his neck over his shoulder, then he'd do it. Take the Helsinki picture, for example.

It's one of the only things Nana had brought with her from her old country. She had to travel light, she said. The advert told them their new husbands would provide for them. 'Wives needed,' it said. She was sixteen years old.

So she brought a picture of a cathedral in Helsinki. She'd bought it as she was waiting for her boat on the wharves of the city. She'd only been there once before – to visit an uncle when she was six – and, now, to leave. The cathedral was built of bright white bricks and had a huge, blue-green dome on top, dotted with painted golden stars. Above it the sky was an almost perfect blue, and so it looked as though one kind of sky was reaching up into another, changing from one of those northern summer nights, where it's never quite dark, into the clearest of days. It was the last building she looked at before the boat pulled away, Nana said, so she was happy she had the picture. And glancing at it now I could see why that was. It looked so still and quiet and clear, so full of light, that it made you feel it'd be there forever. A sky with no clouds. Stars that would always shine.

But whatever Dad saw in it was plain dark. Whenever he looked at it he'd stop whatever he was doing and sit down and stare miserably in front of him as if it were some special place he missed most in the whole world, even though he'd only been there one time ever, on his honeymoon. My dad's circle of tempers was all skewy and seemed to spin around in one direction mostly: down.

I wasn't sure what a circle of tempers was back then, not exactly, but I'd heard Dr Gashinski tell Nana that my dad suffered from something that sounded like cycle diarrhoea, which only made me think of water and shit swirling around in a flushing toilet. She didn't know what it was neither and so he told her it was a Latin word that translated as a circle of tempers, which meant a real up-and-downness in how you felt and that sometimes it'd be like night for my dad and sometimes it'd be like day, except that mostly it seemed like it was night. Virgil would have said that it was like fish and how you could divide them into evening biters and morning biters, except that a bunch of the time my dad wasn't any kind of biter at all: he'd just lie in bed and leave the cups of coffee and plates of pancakes Nana sent me up the stairs with – to tempt him to get up – on the floor beside him.

Don't look back. I do sort of believe that. If it's going to set your circle of tempers spinning any which way, spinning you right down into the dark or the night or the toilet bowl, then don't do it. But stuff comes back when you least expect it. Like Clarence's castle. You never know what you're going to catch when you cast. And if I didn't look back, just a bit, just now and again, then I wouldn't be able to see Virgil, or Dad, or Nana, or Curious George, or any of them. And sometimes I've got no choice but to look that way, just the same as King Lot and those country singers. I can't help it – even if sometimes it leaves a sad, scary taste in my mouth. Backwards is where the lost things are. And where else are you going to find them?

Where the Lost Things Are

It was late in May the day George McKenzie went missing and I knew from the start they were looking in the wrong places.

I was sleeping on the porch because it was one of the first warm days of the year and I was woken up by the sound of knocking at our front door.

'Hello there, Gracie,' Virgil croaked.

Gracie didn't say anything.

'Christ, it's barely morning.'

Gracie started sobbing. The skin on her face scrunched up like it'd got old already, even though she was still young then.

'He's gone, Virgil,' she sobbed. 'He didn't come home.'

'Who's gone? Joseph?'

'No, not Joseph. Don't I wish. Not Joseph.'

'Who, Gracie?'

'It's George.'

I was good and awake then and listened as Virgil started phoning around. Soon I could hear all sorts of people in our kitchen. Jake Ottertale the trapper and Jim Clement and all sorts of other people.

'You take the tracks,' Virgil said to Dad. 'You and Larry. Check as far as the narrows, at least. Me, Jim and Jake'll take the bush as far as Eye Lake. I'll knock at Buddy's and see if he's got a plane free.'

Then it was quiet again and when I walked into the kitchen there was just Nana and Gracie there. Gracie was sitting at the table staring at a napkin and Nana was trying to give her a bowl of porridge with raisins in it, which was what she did when bad things happened.

'Why don't you go outside, Eli,' Nana said. 'We'll get your breakfast later.'

Outside in the garden I found Billy leaning over the fence looking excited and kind of pleased with himself.

'Have you heard?' he said. 'The wolves got George.'

'No they didn't,' I said. 'They just started looking for him.'

'I bet you the wolves got him. They can eat someone in a couple of minutes. Guts and everything.'

'Wolves don't eat people,' I said. 'Except when they're dead.'

'What do you know?' Billy sneered. 'Maybe he is dead.'

Billy's two days older than me and always tried to act like it was years instead, like he knew a hundred times more stuff than me. But he didn't know where George was. Nobody did – except me. But that was eighteen years ago and we were only eleven.

Everyone in our house called George 'Curious George'. We hadn't always called him that and we didn't call him it to his face. We started it when his dad, Joseph McKenzie, lost his job and decided George was allergic to everything and shouldn't go out too much, even to play; which was bad news for me because George was my best friend and when he wasn't around there was usually only me and Billy. Billy lived next door and George lived right across the street, in the only house that was across our street. Beyond us there was just the river and the train tracks and the woods.

You would've thought Mr McKenzie would have noticed George being allergic to everything before and how he was no different than he'd always been – so white and pale he was almost see-through, with eyes that were nearly pink and went red and runny when the sun got too strong. Billy found a word out for it once: albino. He was pretty pleased with himself to start with but lost interest after saying it about a hundred times. But Mr McKenzie decided it was all on account of allergies. It was like the moment he stopped working was the first moment he'd stopped to think about it.

And you would have thought he would have come up with a better explanation. He was a teacher, after all, and educated. Maybe that was why he took losing his job in such a bad way, even though everyone else was losing their jobs too.

Because even back then everything was always closing in Crooked River. People were always talking about how there used to be the railroad and there used to be the lumber mill and there used to be the mine – until it seemed like a town where everything used to be. You'd hear them on the street saying things like, 'This town is finished' and, 'That's it for here – this place is kaput.' Then they'd suddenly begin saying, 'But I tell you, I'm not leaving. I'm from here and I'm not going anywhere!' But some of them must have gone somewhere. Every time George and me went to the corner store to buy comics Mr Krishka, the owner, used to look at us a little sadly and say, 'When I opened this place it used to be 6750.' And I'd feel kind of guilty then, for being 5671. And that was why Mr McKenzie lost his job: because there were less children, just like there was less good lumber and less iron ore and less trains.

When things went kaput for Mr McKenzie he did two things: he decided George was allergic to everything and he started building a higher fence around his house. He started building it in the fall of the year George went missing. I remember that because it was the same fall I thought George and me wouldn't be able to be in the same class any more, on account of the cord that was wrapped around my neck when I was born. And maybe on account of the cold too, though nobody was so sure about that.

I was born in the kitchen of number one O'Callaghan Street – right in the next room – where my mum could be nearest the wood stove. She would have been in the hospital except the tyres had frozen on my dad's truck. It was forty degrees below zero outside. According to my nana I came out completely purple as if I were freezing to death already, but really it was because I had my cord wrapped around my neck and couldn't breathe, not for ages, not until Dr Gashinski cut it with a pair of scissors.

I would've thrown him back, a sickly minnow like that, Virgil used to joke; and sometimes I did imagine myself that day, all purple and gasping for breath like a fish on the bottom of a boat. Later, when I'd hear Nana tell the story of my birth, she'd sometimes give a little shiver, as if it were still forty below outside.

I'd heard Nana telling our teacher, Mrs Arnold, the story that August. I was meant to be in the garden but I was on the porch instead, looking through a crack in the door. Mrs Arnold was sitting in front of a teacup, pushing a piece of her hair back behind her ear and nodding.

'Yes,' she said. 'I understand.'

Nana was explaining about the cord.

Then she said she'd go fetch me and I ran out into the garden.

Seeing as I'd had so much fun that year in school, Mrs Arnold told me, they were going to let me do it again. Aren't you lucky, Eli, Nana said. But I didn't feel lucky. I felt mad and out of breath as if the cord were wrapped around my neck again. On the stove I could see a pot of porridge bubbling. The next week I heard Billy telling George that his mum said I couldn't be in the same grade as them because I was so dumb. But it turned out that even if I had been in the same grade as George we still wouldn't have been in the same class, the same school even, because George never went back to school at all.

The fall came on slow that year. The leaves took a long time to change and drop. There were a few yellow ones on the poplars by the river on our first day back and I noticed a few on the maples outside the museum that were turning red and dying and hanging off like scabs. Billy and me walked past them every day on the way to school and every day there were a few more. But George wasn't with us then. Apparently he was suddenly so allergic he couldn't go to school.

After three weeks of George not coming to school Mrs Arnold came to visit his house. The leaves on the poplars by the river were almost all yellow by then and the wind made them rustle with that dry, flickering sound they have and some of them were falling into the water. I was sitting on the bank, watching them fall and float away on the current. It was always so peaceful down there by the river, watching the water and wondering if there were fish swimming underneath between the weeds. Except it wasn't quite as peaceful that day because Mr McKenzie was sawing planks in his garden to build his fence higher with. He'd been doing it all week – muttering about people interfering and spying, and drinking cans of Molson and sawing up planks and building his fence so high you couldn't see over it. He'd been growing a beard, which was red and full of sawdust, and it reminded me of Noah in the Bible, building his Ark, which we'd been told about in school before they decided I was stupid on account of the cord having been wrapped around my neck. When I saw Mrs Arnold I wanted to run over and tell her how I'd remembered about Noah – just to show her I wasn't completely stupid. I waved and started running but she didn't see me and carried on walking up to the gate of Mr McKenzie's fence, with the wind blowing and a piece of grey hair sticking out from under her hat.

Instead I crept into our garden and from behind the crab apple tree you could hear bits and pieces of what they were saying.

'Let's be reasonable here, Joseph,' Mrs Arnold said. 'The school will take any precautions necessary . . . it's best . . .'

'Do you know what I think's best . . . I'll tell you . . .'

'There's no need to speak to me like that, Joseph . . .'

'And I'll tell you this, Frances . . . if you think the board can throw me aside like an . . . it's all going to shit, to fucking shit, and now I've got to explain myself to you . . . and how long have you even been here, eh, Frances, you fucking out-of-towners thinking you know . . .'

Mostly the conversation seemed to be Mr McKenzie telling Mrs Arnold *this* and then telling her it again and again – with bits of sawdust flying off his beard like flecks of spit – about how everything had gone to shit and how she'd only moved to Crooked River ten years before and so didn't know shit, as if you needed to live in Crooked River for at least twenty years like him to know shit. And Mrs Arnold just being quiet and patient and looking at Mr McKenzie like maybe he needed holding back a grade or two.

This went on for a while. Nana's face was in the window; Virgil was out hunting; Dad was still in his bed. Then suddenly Mr McKenzie turned around and walked back into the house and because Mrs Arnold stayed where she was I thought he was going to get George, to prove how allergic he was to everything, but instead he came out with his deer rifle. He didn't point it, he just held it.

'I think this conversation is over, Frances,' he said. He was talking quietly now.

'I guess it is, Joseph,' Mrs Arnold said.

That's when George started having what they called 'home schooling'. Billy and me were a bit envious at first, thinking now he didn't have to go to school he'd be able to do whatever he wanted during the week. But it didn't work out like that. He wasn't allowed out at all during the week, even after school hours; he was only allowed out on the weekends. The McKenzies' fence was nearly six feet high by then and sometimes we'd see him looking out through gaps in its planks, desperate to see what was going on, all white-faced and wide-eyed like a lemur in a zoo. And that's when we started calling him 'Curious George', after a toy monkey I'd had who was called that.

'Nothing,' my dad shrugged when Virgil got back. Virgil hadn't even asked anything, he'd just looked at him when he came in the door. 'What about you?'

'Nothing.'

'Did Buddy send out a plane?'

'He sent one. But there's only so much you can spot from up there. It's like looking for a needle in the proverbial.'

'How far you get?'

'We did the whole south shore of Eye Lake. We'll do the north tomorrow.'

'Was Joseph with you?'

'Joseph,' Virgil said, stopping and letting the name

linger in the air for a second, as if he were considering it. 'Joseph . . . is a useless lunatic piece of shit. He's not fit to have a son.'

I was sitting in the corner of the kitchen, near the wood stove. Dad turned to me and said, 'Don't worry, Eli. We'll find him. Tomorrow, we'll find him tomorrow.'

It was strange then, how for a second Dad and Virgil seemed to have changed places: how Dad was hopeful but Virgil looked tired and sad.

I don't know why we hadn't thought of the name Curious George before. It suited him just perfect. George was good at finding things – better than me, better than Billy, better than Virgil and Dad, better than anybody. He always had been. To some eyes the bush around Crooked River probably seemed pretty empty; the sort of place you pass on highways, counting down kilometres, watching the lakes and forests and swamps go by, thinking there's nothing there, that it all looks the same. But it isn't like that. Take a step or two off the road, go into the trees, and you'll find all kinds of stuff: abandoned trappers' shacks, burnt-out trucks, tins, cans, bottles, old arrowheads, drill bits, bits of engines, bags of garbage. The sort of stuff that once it was there long enough would become historical like our old wood stove and the basement things and get put in the museum.

Whenever George found something good he'd come over the street and wait for me outside our porch, shifting from one foot to the other, smiling a bit in his sideways way with his hands shoved tight in his pockets as if he had it hidden right there. But it wouldn't be hidden there; it'd already be in his room with the rest of his 'Exhibits'.

George's 'Exhibits' took up two whole walls of his room. They sat on shelves, with little cardboard signs taped to the wood under each one to tell you what they were. It's a long time since I saw them, but these are the ones I remember:

An owl's egg, still in the nest
An otter's skull
Five bear's teeth
A small box full of spent shotgun cartridges
A rusty axe head
A Fifties-style cartoon picture of two hunters in a
    snowy woods, with a third hidden behind a tree
    trying to have a shit. 'Listen,' says one to the other,
    'I think I heard a buck snort.'
Some beer caps, flattened by passing trains
An old boot
Two ancient snowshoes

There were others too, lots of others. I wish I could remember them. George used to dust them himself every week – he wouldn't let Gracie do it – but you can't dust the inside of your head, even though a kind of dust does seem to fall and settle there over the years, like snow, covering some things but leaving others plain in view.

When George went looking for new exhibits he called it going on expeditions. Gracie had got him a subscription to *National Geographic* for his eighth birthday and he spent plenty of time peering through those yellow-edged magazines. I think he thought he was just like the people who took pictures and wrote in it, exploring and finding things in faraway places. The bush looked different when you were with George: it was never only the bush and it was never empty.

It was a morning early in October – it must have been a Saturday morning because I wasn't in school and Nana hadn't gone to church – that I saw George standing outside our porch. His smile was bigger and more lopsided than usual. He was hopping from foot to foot like a heron. In the kitchen I heard Virgil telling Dad, 'There's a cat that just got the cream!'

'What you get?' I asked.

'Come on, I'll show you.'

I thought we were going to go over the road to his house but instead George carried on towards the river.

'Quick,' he said. 'Before Billy comes out.'

We followed the river for about half a mile, past the two old white pines, until we came to a bunch of scrubby willow trees. Down here, said George, and we scrabbled between them until we got to where the cattails and bulrushes grew and the earth squelched and gave and came up over our ankles. The water had cooled through September and it chilled our toes. Between the rushes there was a line of red, as bright and deep as the turning maples. See, George said, and after a few seconds I could. There was an old canoe lying upside down on the sludge.

'Whose is that?'

'I think it's my dad's. I saw him come here last week and use it.'

'For what?'

'For his research.'

Mr McKenzie had been going off into the bush for a few years. Nobody knew where exactly, and they weren't sure why neither – he didn't ever come back with fish or dead animals. Sometimes he went in the evenings after he finished at the school, other times he went for a whole weekend; now he wasn't working at the school I suppose he went more often. Whenever I asked George why he said it was for his dad's research, but I never knew what he researched and George never said. He taught geography so I thought maybe it was rocks, like the ones he showed us about in school – the chunks of haematite and granite and amethyst that sat on shelves in his classroom (we learnt a lot about rocks, because we were sat on one big one – the Shield). Or I thought maybe he was helping Gracie out by trying to find historical stuff for the museum. Everyone else thought he was staking claims: nobody told you what they were doing or where they were going when they did that.

'We can take it tomorrow for an expedition.'

'What about your dad?' I asked. I'd always been a bit scared of Mr McKenzie at school and now everyone was getting a bit scared of him too, because of the fence and the home schooling and everything.

'He's in Thunder Bay tomorrow. He won't know.'

*

George wore a funny hat the next day. It was made of straw and had a wide, flat brim. 'It's to keep the sun off my eyes,' he told me. But the sun was getting weak by then and staying lower and lower against the horizon. I reckoned it was the kind of hat he thought the people from *National Geographic* wore.

We set off straight after lunch, carrying fishing rods so everyone would think we were headed for the railway bridge. We fished a lot there when we were kids, casting red and white bobbers out into the middle of the stream and letting them drift and settle in the pools behind the steel pylons, where the water looked stillest. But even there the current would sometimes play tricks, nibbling on our hooks and tugging at the bobbers the same as fish.

It played tricks with the canoe too. I sat in the stern and tried to steer, but the water kept swirling slowly one way and then another until in the end I just let it take us wherever it wanted to. Up ahead in the bow George was trying to paddle, except the paddle was too big for his skinny arms and he was only dipping it in the water, letting it taste the surface like a big tongue. Sometimes he'd make little speeches about what was happening as we went along, as if he were writing in a diary or a piece for the *National Geographic*:

Rounding the second bend Eli and I passed a stand of poplars and a beaver lodge. The river widened here until it was about fifteen feet wide and the bulrushes grew thickly along its edges. There were animal tracks along the far bank that we couldn't properly identify; Eli suggested moose but I felt sure they were bear. We decided to proceed with extra caution.

Our route took us west. All rivers this side of the watershed flow north to the Arctic Sea. Fifty miles east of us, on the other side of the watershed, all rivers flow south to the Atlantic Ocean. Neither Eli or I are exactly sure why this is – Eli commented that water is like a dog and knows where it's supposed to go – but I shall consult my books about this on our return in order to find out a more – how shall I put it – scientific explanation.

Some three kilometres into our expedition the river narrowed so much that overhanging spruce boughs began to interfere with my headgear. Eli was having problems keeping our craft in the middle of the channel. Through the trees I could make out signs of recent activity, animal most probably: saplings pushed down on their sides; branches chewed. Beaver? Possibly moose. Possibly bear. I felt it better to keep further out from the shore and informed Eli of this. He said he was doing the best he could and maybe I should navigate if I thought it was so damn easy.

After probably six kilometres, maybe more, Eli decided to take a rest. We drifted close to the shore. Eli saw a muskrat but I only saw its tail. Both of us spotted a moose's antler tangled up in the lily pads and I wanted to keep it as an exhibit except the water was too shallow for us to reach it in the canoe. Further in from the shore, past the swampy bits, there was an outcrop of bare rock covered in light green and orange lichen. Nobody had written anything on it like they usually do near town, but that's because nobody from town comes out here.

Or so we thought. No more than twenty feet from where he saw the muskrat, Eli found a set of tracks at the edge of the river. These tracks were almost certainly *homo sapiens* – they were made with boots. We landed the canoe and decided to investigate this further, on foot.

I thought George was going to disappear into the swamp when we got out of the canoe: he went straight through the bog mat and the water slurped right up over his knees. He insisted on going in front of me, pulling himself along from one clump of reeds and grass to the next, and when he got a bit ahead the back of his neck was a little white dot in the green, like a swamp flower.

The tracks were quite new and easy to follow, even though they shouldn't have been there: people from town didn't go in this direction much – there weren't any good fishing lakes nearby or logging roads or anything really. Maybe a hunter or two might come this time of year, looking for moose, or some prospectors, looking for iron ore and gold and any other stuff they hoped might be there. The bush was full of old mining shafts that'd been abandoned and forgotten. Every few years, when people got excited or desperate, mostly desperate, they'd swarm out into the woods and fill it with holes like mosquito bites. Keep one eye on the ground wherever else you got the other one pointed, is what Virgil always told me.

I kept one eye on the ground and the other on George. He followed the tracks up over an outcrop of rock and into the trees beyond. They were harder to see there, in the beds of moss and pine needles and fallen leaves, so he waited for me.

'What do you think?' he asked. 'Which way?'

'I don't know. I can't see nothing.'

'After consulting with Eli, I decided to head northwards where there was what looked like a clearing in the trees.'

It was hardly a clearing but you could tell a few trees had been downed: the sun was falling straight through onto the saplings and the moss had shrivelled away. I rooted around until I found some stumps. They'd been sawed, not chewed.

'Somebody cut this,' I yelled over to George, who was standing on the other side peering into some blueberry bushes.

'Eli,' he said, and I could barely hear him his voice was so low. 'Eli, you better come see this.' He wasn't talking in his *National Geographic* voice no more.

When I started walking he hissed: 'Watch your feet! Watch where you're stepping!'

'I got one eye on the ground,' I said.

George was looking straight into the teeth of a bear trap. It was one of the real old kind, the ones they weren't supposed to use any more, and was sitting there beneath a blueberry bush – two big wide-open jaws covered with rusty teeth, waiting for something to step on it and make it smile.

'I almost stepped on it,' George whispered. You could tell he was thinking about what would've happened if he had. I had a pretty good idea myself. I'd found one in our basement once and Billy had got me to set it, for an experiment, and stick a piece of two-by-four into it. It'd jumped shut on that wood like a starving animal; the teeth went in at least two inches. Dad had taken it to the dump afterwards.

After looking at it for a minute or two George must have got it into his head he wanted it for an exhibit. We could put a stick in it, he said. And so I did, even though I knew what would happen on account of the one in our basement. It went through a whole poplar sapling when it snapped and George looked down at his leg for a second; he was having a second thought or two about keeping it. We were a whole bunch more careful exploring the clearing after that.

Right in the middle of it there was a place where the ground rose up into a big hump, the same shape as earth when it's heaped on a grave. There were only a few tufts of grass growing on top and George thought it might be one of those Indian burial mounds. He got real excited about that, what with all the exhibits that might be inside, and started digging into it there and then with his hands; they were so white against the dirt they looked like bones already, like we really were digging in a grave. I didn't much feel like doing that myself so I just kicked the sides of it with my boot.

But it was my boot that found it. The first few kicks were against dirt but the third was against something hard and made a hollow noise.

'What's that?' George said, poking his head up. In his ears it must've sounded like a box of treasure. It wasn't. It was a door.

I never wanted to open that door. There was an inch or so of dirt covering it and I would've been happy enough leaving it there. But beneath the brim of his hat George's eyes were almost popping out of their sockets, as if they couldn't wait and were trying to see right through it. You would've thought we were about to go into a pyramid or something. But in the end it was me who had to pull it open: George wasn't strong enough even though the hinges were well oiled. The air from inside came out cool and clean-smelling, like metal – which wasn't what we'd expected. There were wooden steps going down into where it was dark.

We were both scared. I'm not embarrassed or nothing to admit that. I wouldn't have gone a step further if it'd just been me. But if you liked finding things as much as George did, if you badly wanted to find them, then you had to go places you didn't really want to go, even the ones that scared you. It was part of the deal. George went down the steps first and I followed him.

We couldn't see nothing at first, could only hear our voices go out into the dark space and touch its sides and come back to us. It seemed bigger than it looked from above. And then our eyes got used to it and we could see corners and edges and things beside us. There were tall metal shelves, reaching up above our heads to the ceiling and then stretching away to where we couldn't see; there was the back of a chair and the side of a table, with a piece of paper curling over it; there was a kind of cylinder hanging from the roof that George banged his head on – it knocked his hat off, swung forwards, and then swung back. He reached up and grabbed it, turning to me, hatless, with his face as white as a moth's wing in the darkness.

'I think it's a flashlight,' he whispered.

'Then turn it on,' I said.

'That's what I'm trying to do.'

It *was* bigger than it looked from above. The sides were bare earth studded with rocks, and the ceiling was made out of boards.

There were four rows of shelves, mostly stacked with cans. George and me walked along them one by one, telling each other what kind we saw.

'Green beans.'

'Ham.'

'Corn.'

'Tomatoes.'

And so on. But there was lots of other stuff apart from the cans. We found pots and pans, matches, knives, coils of rope, boxes of freeze-dried food, axes, nails, bullets – pretty much everything you could think of. Two hunting rifles and a shotgun sat on a rack by the door.

The paper spread out on the table was a map of Canada and America. Somebody had drawn a bunch of little red circles on it, mostly around cities in America, and connected them with lines to Crooked River. They made the map look like a huge red spider's web, and there were numbers beside every line, saying how many kilometres it was from each circle to Crooked River; the closest ones had a second, much bigger, circle around them – but none of them quite touched the tiny blue squiggle of the Crooked River.

I don't know how long we were down there – maybe ten or fifteen minutes, maybe half an hour, it was hard to tell. It seemed like time had got stuck or stretched or something, the way the dust moved slow, barely falling, through the beams of the flashlight that hung from the ceiling, still rocking gently back and forth from when George had knocked it with his head; as if one movement could last a hundred years down there, could keep on going and going and going like a clock that keeps ticking even when there's no more time to tell. It was like being in a kind of trance or dream and it wasn't till we stepped back into the place where the light came in from the door that it broke. There were ravens croaking up above and a long chick-ka-dee-dee-deee drifted in from the woods. The world was out there with things living and moving in it, things we'd almost forgotten to think about.

'Do you think someone lives here?' George suddenly said.

'I don't know. I reckon . . .'

'Do you think it's a shacker?'

You won't see any mention of them in the museum but when we were kids there were still some shackers about, the same as there still used to be caribou about when the old-timers were kids. Or maybe you would find something about them somewhere in the museum, but Mr Haney wouldn't call them shackers, he'd call them 'characters'. There'd be a picture on the wall and underneath it a name with 'a real character' written beside it in brackets. I never knew what the difference was exactly. Shackers were just guys who lived out in the bush by themselves – in shacks.

Some of them did a bit of trapping and a few did some prospecting, but mostly you didn't really know what they did. They minded their own business and everyone else minded it too. You didn't see them in town much, which was the whole purpose of being a shacker I guess: if you lived in the bush you must've wanted to be alone, because that's what you'd be about ninety-nine per cent of the time.

I suppose one difference was there were ones it was OK to say hello and talk to if you saw them and others you were meant to stay good and clear of. For instance there was the Earl, who used to live right on the shore of Eye Lake, no more than a couple of hundred yards from where I lived. He was an Englishman, old and short and skinny, who wore thick glasses and spoke like he was the Queen's husband. It was fine to say hello to the Earl, if he ever came out of his shack; not that you'd expect him to say hello back or anything – mostly he talked to himself or his invisible friends and didn't want to be interrupted. (Sometimes Virgil stopped for a drink with him when he went fishing, but that was the exception.) Then there was Oskar the Finn, who lived a-ways down the tracks. You weren't supposed to even look at Oskar. Nobody ever said anything exactly, but you were meant to keep a good rifle's shot of distance between him and you if you did see him. We kids all got the idea he'd slit peoples' throats or eaten babies or something worse (Billy had a bunch of ideas). The Earl was a character; Oskar was a plain shacker.

'It could be,' I said to George, and we looked at each

other for a bit, all hushed and breathless, probably thinking of throats being slit and babies being eaten. George's eyes were beginning to water around the edges. They did that from the sun, or sometimes from when he was excited or scared or thinking hard about something. Right then you could tell he was excited *and* scared *and* thinking hard.

'I reckon we should get,' I said. There was something about that place that made me not want to be there.

George's eyes watered some more. He was looking back and forth from the light at the door to the stuff on the shelves, moving his weight from foot to foot the same as when he'd found stuff and stood outside our porch. I knew he wanted to go and he didn't want to go all at once. And I knew as well that we'd be coming back. It was the most stuff he'd ever found.

On our way to the canoe I kept two eyes on the ground. I didn't want to find nothing more. I wished George wasn't so curious.

By the end of the third day they still hadn't found George. Every morning the men gathered in our kitchen before they set off, eating bowls of Nana's porridge, checking maps, and talking about where they were headed. Every time they crossed off a section of a map they talked a little less.

'This is beginning to feel like Dad all over again,' I heard my dad say.

'Don't I know it,' Virgil replied sadly, looking out the window. 'It's the Bermuda Triangle,' he said.

The Bermuda Triangle

One of the first times I saw the Earl he was wandering about in his pyjamas talking to himself. Or if he was talking to someone then I sure couldn't see them. Virgil had taken me to Eye Lake to go fishing and we were at the boat launch, getting ready to set off, when I spotted the Earl outside the door of his shack pacing back and forth in his slippers. 'This,' he kept on saying, spreading his arms out in front of him, 'this is my Bermuda Triangle.' When I asked Virgil what he meant he said the Bermuda Triangle was a place in the Atlantic Ocean where things went missing – like ships and planes and people – and were never found. Then why's the outside of his door the Bermuda Triangle, I asked? Has he lost something there? Not exactly, said Virgil. I think it's him who's a little lost. I didn't really understand that. When I asked why the Earl was wearing his pyjamas and talking to himself Virgil said it was a free country and it was no business of ours if a man wanted to walk about in his pyjamas and enjoy his own conversation. But after that, whenever I couldn't find something, or lost a lure, Virgil would say, 'It's the Bermuda Triangle.'

The Bermuda Triangle was where I imagined my grandfather was. I couldn't imagine exactly what it looked like there but I was pretty sure you could have your own version of it, like the Earl did. And in my head my grandfather's version was quite a bit like the Crooked River, except looped into a big circle – somewhere with no watershed at all, where he paddled around and around without getting anywhere.

Because the last thing anybody saw of Clarence O'Callaghan was a set of footprints leading away into the bush east of Eye Lake and along the banks of the Crooked River. Some people said there were two sets of footprints going into the bush and one coming back; others said there was just the one and none coming back, but to tell the truth I couldn't tell you what was there. Clarence took those steps fifteen years before I was born. They were washed away before I was even a twinkle and all he left behind for me was this picture I have – not like the one of him in the photo or anything, but in my mind and sometimes in my dreams – of him walking down to the river through the trees, slipping in and out of view until at last he's out of sight, somewhere my eyes can't find him. I can't tell if he's reached the river and I can't ever be sure if he's really gone or not. In the picture he's always there and never there. He could walk back any second but he never does. They didn't ever find a body, not a single bone.

And that was all – until I found his castle.

I must have been sitting in the living room for hours, leafing through Dad and Virgil's records, before I decided to go down into the basement to look at Clarence's things.

I'm not sure why I went there – it'd always been the one place in number one O'Callaghan Street I was afraid of – but it was like once I'd started looking back I couldn't help myself. I had to look further and further. I had to follow the footprints.

When I was a kid there was nowhere worse than the basement. I think it was the noises mostly. During the day Nana would do our laundry there in an old washing machine: a huge, rust-streaked white cube with a big steel mouth that opened at the top. You could hear it all through the house, quaking and shuddering as it digested our clothes. Its appetite was enormous and often Nana would spend whole mornings and afternoons dragging piles of our clothes down the steps to it like she was taking them to a monster to be sacrificed. She kept a washboard beside the machine and a mangle too, that looked like the pictures of torture contraptions in dungeons that were in one of Virgil's history books, and if I went too close to the steps I'd hear the wet, muffled cries of the laundry being racked and strangled in the shadows below. And then at night the stove would judder into life and terrible gurgling and groaning sounds would come up through the heating pipes into my bedroom. They were the voices of the shapeless things I was sure lived in the basement and only came out at night, the same as skunks and raccoons, and roasted their victims in the flames of the stove. I imagined them hunched in the corners of the room, or hidden behind the pipes, whispering to each other in the darkness. And whispering to me too, trying to persuade me to come join them, because sometimes I'd find myself awake in the middle of the night, standing at the top of the steps, my eyes blinking open from sleepwalk and staring right down into that whispering darkness.

Sometimes even when something stops it keeps on going, and walking down those steps it was as if I could still hear the machine rumbling away and the sounds of Nana squelching my wet clothes on the washboard. But when I got to the bottom there was nothing there except quietness, the heavy quietness of places that have been empty for a long while. The stove was gone but the machine was still there – they didn't want that at the museum – and the mangle too. I pictured Nana's hands turning its handle, her raw-wet fingers clasped hard against the wood, knuckles worn red – red like the dots you see when you press your eyelids closed – turning and turning it as though her old body would never run out of strength, washing everything as clean and bright as the Helsinki sky.

Nana had put all of Clarence's things in a big travelling trunk; the old-fashioned kind people use in black-and-white films when they take cruises, with labels on them saying all the places they've been. It made it look like he'd forgotten his luggage, or just got back from a trip and put it down; like you might expect to find a new label on it saying 'Nowhere' or 'The Bush' or 'The Bermuda Triangle'.

When I opened the trunk there were no surprises. It'd been years and years since I'd opened it before but everything was still there, the same as I remembered it:

There was Clarence's pistol: a German Luger he'd bought from someone after the war. Virgil used to bring it fishing with us sometimes – to shoot slubes off the end of his line when he didn't want to bring them in the boat.

There was the sign that used to hang on the front of Clarence's hotel before I was born. *The Pioneer Hotel*, it said.

There was a map, a real old one, with lots of blank green and blue spaces and a black X marking the spot where Crooked River would have been, if it had existed yet.

There was a worn, slightly crumpled invitation to a dance at the Pioneer Hotel, signed 'Clarence O'Callaghan. Proprietor'. On the back was a scribbled note that I could never quite work out the words of.

There was Clarence's fiddle.

There was an envelope, addressed to somewhere in Chicago, with *addressee unknown/return* stamped overtop of it and our address on the back. Inside it was the photo of Clarence standing beside his castle.

And that was all. It wasn't much.

Of course once upon a time there'd been his clothes and tools and stuff too, but every year he hadn't come back Nana had given bits and pieces of those away until, before I was around, they were gone. I guess they weren't that important. Apparently these – the things that still remained – were the only things Clarence would've kept no matter what. So Nana stored them in the trunk, as if he might walk back in at any moment and say, 'Where's my luggage? I must've forgot it.'

*

The first thing I decided to do when I got back to the Poplars was take Bobby minnow fishing. I went to the Tamarack dorm to pick up some pins and line and then headed straight to the Pine dorm. Sarah was outside, putting in her screen windows. She was wearing a pair of overalls, covered in splotches of paint, and an orange baseball cap that said Red Head, even though her hair wasn't red at all – it was black.

'Hey there,' I said, and for some reason I thought I'd better try and make a joke. 'You steal that from a real redhead?'

She looked a bit confused at first but then she smiled.

'Oh this,' she laughed. 'I think it's an old duck-hunting hat.'

And sure enough there was a little picture of a duck right under the writing. She kept smiling and I would've liked to make another joke but I couldn't think of any.

'Is Bobby around?' I asked. 'I thought he might like to go minnow fishing or something.'

She smiled even more then, as if I had made another joke.

'Of course, Eli. He'd love that.'

'I wasn't going to use proper hooks or nothing, just bent pins – to get him started.'

'That's very considerate of you, Eli. I'll just get him ready.'

I liked the way Sarah spoke in different ways: some-times polite and proper and then other times like most everybody else in Crooked River. Her father was an engin-eer and her family had only moved here when she was already sixteen or so. And then they'd moved on because there wasn't much need for engineers in Crooked River any more, but she'd stayed because of Billy.

Bobby came out of the Pine dorm wearing his sheets and we started off down the path to the shoreline. As soon as we were out of sight he took off the sheets and stashed them behind a rock.

'I'm sick of wearing them,' he said.

'That's OK,' I said, 'I won't tell. You want some bug dope?'

'I'm not supposed to use it,' he said. 'Mum says it gives you cancer.'

I took Billy along the shore to where the old dock was, near the boat launch. The Earl used to live about a hundred yards further on along the shore and if you looked a few feet back in the bush there was a pile of boards that used to be his shack. (When they first made the conference centre it'd still been standing and they'd put a sign on it saying *Traditional Trapper's Cabin*.)

Bobby was asking me about a hundred questions at once – about why this was a good spot and why we weren't using proper hooks and a whole bunch of other questions like that. I tried to slow him down and answer them as best I could.

I told him minnows were just the same as bigger fish. They liked living beside things, like rocks or logs or reefs or old docks, so they could hide from other fish that were trying to eat them. 'If you're a minnow you don't want to spend too much time in the open water where everything can see you,' I told him. 'It's dangerous. You want to find yourself a bit of cover.' Then I bent a couple of pins in half and showed Bobby how to tie the line onto them. I told him pins were fine for minnows and we'd get onto barbed hooks when he'd had a bit of practice.

'And reels and rods too?'

'Yes, and reels and rods too,' I said.

'Why do you need barbs?' he asked.

'To keep a fish on when you've set it.'

'What's setting?'

'It's when you give your line a little tug to get the hook stuck in its mouth.'

'What's the bacon for?'

'It's for bait,' I said, and cut us each a tiny piece of white fat for putting on our hooks.

I hadn't fished for minnows since I was Bobby's age or younger. It was strange how having him with me made it feel as if I was doing it for the first time myself and was that age all over again. I could feel that hopeful beating of my heart as I looked over the side into the water, the what's-in-there flutter of the blood that every fisherman starts out with and never leaves behind, not really.

We lay down on our bellies and leaned over the edge of the dock, holding our lines in our hands.

'Now put her into the water,' I told Bobby.

'How will I know when I got one?'

'You just wait till you can't see the bacon fat. When you see it disappear give your line a jerk.'

'So when I *can't* see it, I got something?'

'That's it, Bobby. When it looks like it's gone then you'll probably have one biting.'

I dropped my line in near Bobby's and watched the white fleck of bacon fat drift down towards the cradle of the dock, where everything was shadowy and murky. Sometimes it looked like there might be something moving through the water, a shape like a minnow's back or fin, but then it'd turn into shadow again. Bobby had stopped asking questions the moment his line went in. He was staring at his hook all hushed and expectant, the same as me, and everything was quiet, more quiet than the air can be – like we'd become part of the still, waiting quiet of the underwater. This is what I love about fishing: how it gets like this; like there's nothing but you and your line, no thinking or remembering or nothing; how with my hook in the water there was no difference between me then and me when I was Bobby's age.

Virgil told me once, when he was teaching me to fish, that they called it Eye Lake because down there, on its bed, lay all the people who'd ever drowned in it – the loggers and the fishermen and the unlucky ones who'd gone through the ice in the winters – staring up towards a surface they'd never reach again. He called them the watchers and said they never blinked and that if the water was clear and calm then you might see the whites of their eyes glistening like pearls below you.

'Do they ever sleep?' I asked him.

'No,' he said. 'Never.'

'So what do they do?'

'They look up, Eli. They watch.'

'For what?'

'I don't know, Eli. Maybe for us?'

'Forever?'

'I guess so,' he said kind of sorrowfully. 'I guess so.'

What do they want from us? I always wish I'd asked Virgil that, only I never did. I never got the chance. And suddenly I wasn't seeing the white of the bacon fat in the water; it was them, watching me, unblinking, the whites of their eyes asking me . . .

'What do you want?' I shouted. 'What do you want?'

A streak of wet silver jumped out of the water, catching the sun and glittering. It landed on the planks of the dock and flopped up and down. Behind it was Bobby's face, pale and scared.

'I got one,' he whispered. 'I got one, Eli.'

Behind him I could see Sarah walking towards the dock.

'Is everything OK?' she called over to us. 'I thought I heard shouting.'

Bobby looked at me. The scaredness had gone out of his face and his eyebrows were knotted together as if he were figuring something out. Then he picked his minnow off the dock and ran over to Sarah.

'Look,' he said. 'I got one! I got one!'

'That's great, Bobby,' she said, smiling. 'What happened to your bug clothes?'

'See,' Bobby said breathlessly, as if he'd not heard the question. 'I got one!'

He held out his hand to her and the minnow lay there

in his palm, flopping from side to side, its little mouth opening and closing, gasping for breath.

That evening I walked down Franklin's Trail to the spot where I'd snagged Clarence's castle. I sat on a piece of driftwood by the shoreline and stared out across the water. It was smooth and still and in the distance the dead trees stuck out of its surface. It looked like the remains of a forest fire so hot it had melted the soil to glass. And the setting sun was burning the lake and turning the far shore into a dark outline, sloping gently up and down in the shape of a sleeping giant, and then – for the time of a few breaths – turning the trees behind me a bright golden green, so bright and golden and green they were the colour of fevers.

When I saw it, it was like I knew it'd be there. The tower of the castle, jutting out of the surface. The water seemed to be dropping almost as fast as the sun.

Everything comes back in the end.

Through the woods I could hear shouting and I ran towards it until I got to the Pine dorm. Billy's truck was parked out front and Bobby was standing in the garden, wrapped up in his sheets. There were so many bugs you could hardly breathe, and the sound of them was everywhere, as if they'd flown into my ear and were buzzing around inside my head. Billy's voice sounded like them too, starting slow and faint and then reaching up and up until it became a loud whining. I couldn't tell what he was saying. It all sounded like mosquito to me.

'Mum doesn't want Billy to visit any more,' Bobby whispered.

I didn't say nothing.

'I kept my minnow in a bucket,' Bobby said. 'And I put a rock in there too, for cover. Like you said they liked.'

'I don't want you just turning up, Billy,' I heard Sarah shouting from inside. 'I'm not your fucking fallback when your whores are out of town. Nine years, Billy! Nine fucking years! We're either your family or we're not!'

'That's good,' I said to Bobby. 'They like rocks.'

'Fuck you!' Billy whined. 'This is my family's frigging property, if you've not noticed. And that's my kid.'

'Where you keeping it?' I asked Bobby.

'Down by the lake.'

And I was going to get him to show me it when the door flew open and Billy strode out in a big huff. We looked at each other in what light was still left.

'What the fuck are you doing here, Eli?'

I didn't say nothing. I was thinking how I wished Billy had been number four thousand or something, so I wouldn't have to have grown up with him.

'I mean, what the fuck?'

'Eli came to see the minnow I caught,' Bobby said. 'We went fishing.'

'Now this takes the frigging cookie,' Billy shouted at no one in particular. He was standing in the same way he'd always stood, ever since he was a kid, with his legs bandied out wide like he'd just got off a horse, like he was a cowboy having a tantrum. His new moustache was twitching up and down as if it were an inchworm walking over a leaf. 'Eli-fucking-O'Callaghan. Is that what *this* is? You've got so frigging desperate you've started banging Eli?'

'You're such a spoilt goddam prick,' Sarah said. She was standing in the doorway behind him. Her voice had gone still and calm now. 'As if that'd be any of your business, Billy. Nine years on and off, waiting for you to grow up. As if it'd be your business any more who I banged.'

'Damn fucking right it's my business,' Billy said. 'It's my kid, Sarah. I don't want some frigging retard playing daddy to my kid.'

Sarah's face turned as hard and white as quartz.

'He's not,' she said.

'Not what? Retarded? I've known him my whole fucking life, remember!'

'He's not your kid, Billy.'

Billy turned around and punched her in the face.

'You better go now, Billy,' I said.

Billy said nothing, he just climbed into his truck.

Afterwards I got Bobby to show me his minnow, while Sarah was cleaning up her face. It was too dark to see it in the bottom of the bucket but I pretended I could anyway.

'It's a shiner,' I told him.

'Who were you shouting at?' Bobby asked. 'When we were fishing.'

'Oh,' I said. 'That wasn't nobody.'

Crooked River: Population 1

I don't have a phone but there's one in the office building. When Sarah knocked on my door and said I had a call I wasn't really sure what she was talking about at first – I never get calls; I can't remember ever getting one. I walked with her a bit, towards the office, and there were bruises under both her eyes and a cut across the top of her nose. I didn't know what to say at all.

'Your face looks pretty bad,' I said.

'You know what, Eli,' she said. 'In a strange way I'm glad it does.'

She put her hand up to her cheek and said: 'This is a full stop. This is absolutely a full stop. This ends the whole miserable page.'

The office had a big boulder right in front of it with a sign that said: *This represents the obstacles we can overcome.* There's a bunch of other stuff like that in the grounds of the Poplars – for the business people who never overcame the bugs and snow I guess. There's even a statue of Buddy Bryce that he paid an artist to make. He wasn't that happy when it arrived, though. It didn't look like him at all: it was a mushroom-shaped piece of iron, with a kind of stalk growing out the top. It had a sign explaining it too: *This represents the Northern Spirit. The upward thrust of the sculpture, akin to a new branch growing from a tree, encapsulates the vision, entrepreneurship and endeavour of pioneers like Buddy Bryce.*

I remember when they first showed it. Buddy had invited a bunch of people from town to the Poplars and it was covered in a white sheet. Then the artist – a funny-looking guy with long black hair and glasses – said a few words and pulled off the sheet. Everybody clapped, except for Buddy. He looked like someone had just filled his boots with moose piss.

Afterwards I heard Buddy and the artist talking.

'It doesn't look nothing like me,' Buddy said. 'Jesus! It doesn't look like *anything*.'

'It's figurative,' the artist said. 'It symbolizes your achievements.'

'*Figurative*,' Buddy hissed. 'Well, maybe that thousand bucks I'm supposed to be shelling out for it is figurative too. It symbolizes you trying to rip me off with this piece of junk.'

When I got to the phone I'd started thinking things through and reckoned it was probably going to be Buddy, phoning to sack me. It was going to be a full stop for me too.

It wasn't Buddy though.

At first it sounded like a bad connection, low and raspy and crackling, but it turned out to be Gracie McKenzie and that's just how she sounds.

'Eli,' she said. 'I think you better come to the museum. They found something . . . Are you there, Eli?'

I'd kind of forgotten to say anything, because I wasn't used to getting calls. 'I'm here,' I blurted, and realized I didn't need to talk so loud. 'What they find?'

'Remains,' she said. There was another long pause when I forgot to speak again.

'Look, Eli, I'll tell you everything when you get here. OK?'

'OK,' I said.

On the walk into town I found a baby owl sitting under a jack pine. It was covered in white fluff and stared at me with its black eyes, snapping its beak and opening and closing its talons. Up above in the branches I could hear another, louder, snapping noise, and when I looked I found its mother there, staring angrily down at me with the same fierce, black eyes. I thought I could maybe find the nest and put the baby owl back, but the way its mother was staring at me you could tell that wasn't such a good idea.

When I arrived at the museum Mr Haney was standing outside again, with his hands on his hips, shaking his head. The big poster above the door had come off at the corner and was peeling down. *ENNIAL*, it said. *001*.

'I just can't get it to stay put, Eli,' he said.

Inside, Gracie was sitting in her glass office. She must have been smoking a lot because you could hardly see her in there, the smoke was so thick; some of it drifted out the window of the office into the museum, making everything look grainy and misty. Clarence peered from the wall as if he was trying to spot me through a fog.

When Gracie saw me she waved her hand and I went in and sat on a chair opposite her desk. There were piles of old newspapers strewn over it: copies of the *Crooked River Progress* from years and years back. Here and there you could see a face smiling out from them, some Miss Teen Crooked River or Bass Classic winner from ages ago. Gracie's skin looked like their newspaper skin – thin and yellowy and brittle; from another time.

'I tell you, Eli,' she rasped, 'it'll be another hundred years before I finish cataloguing this junk. Now look, I'm sorry for dragging you all the way here but I thought I'd best tell you about what they found.'

'Who?'

'Some fishermen or canoeists or something. I don't know. It doesn't matter who.'

'What they find?' I asked. My head was beginning to hurt around the temples as though I were wearing a cap that was too small for me. I was hoping she was going to say Clarence's castle and then I'd say it was me who found it and that's why I'd come yesterday – to tell Mr Haney and her. But the pinched, hurting part of my head was thinking something else.

'Remains,' Gracie said. 'Human remains.'

She was looking right at me. Her eyes were glistening and dark like the owl's. They were younger than her face, even though her face was older than she was. I kept my own eyes on the faces of the newspaper people.

'I didn't want to explain all this on the phone, Eli – the details are still a bit loosey-goosey. But they found them east of Eye Lake, near the bank of the Crooked River. One adult male, they said. Not recent.'

One adult male. I'd heard it when she said it, in her voice: a little flinch or flicker of something – of relief, I guess. I felt it too.

'The thing is, I always promised your uncle Virgil if I heard anything about them finding human stuff, anything that might be about Clarence, then I'd tell him first. I promised him, Eli, and you're the closest thing left now so I'm telling you.'

In my mind I could see footprints and the river flowing, around and around. It was soothing in a way. It was the picture I'd always had.

'Of course, this could be nothing to do with your grandfather, nothing at all. The police are nosing through the bones as we speak. They might be in touch with you.'

My head began to hurt again. 'Why?' I asked. 'What do they want with me?'

'For identification, Eli. To get a DNA sample and what not.'

I didn't really get what all that meant but Gracie said it was just the same as in those TV shows where bits of people are like fingerprints and people from the same family have the same ones. By taking a sample of me they could check if the remains were Clarence's.

'I haven't got a TV at the Poplars,' I said. 'I sure wish I did.'

Then I heard Mr Haney making coughing noises outside the office.

'What do you want, Tom?' Gracie said.

'It's just in case of visitors, Grace. There's an awful lot of smoke . . .'

'Jesus, Tom. When the hell was the last time we had visitors?'

Outside the museum there's an old steam train and an old mining drill and an old canoe standing on two poles. I went to sit on the bench beside it. It used to be made of birch bark but that rotted away so they replaced it with plastic. Underneath, a placard says: *This is to commemorate the arrival of Clarence O'Callaghan on the site of what subsequently became the Township of Crooked River.* Before it came to the museum, the canoe used to sit in a shed in our garden and George used to sneak in there sometimes to take a peek at it. Sometimes I'd catch him at the shed door peering at it, tilting his head slowly this way and that, like a curious bird.

The arrival of Clarence was George's favourite story in school. We had normal history lessons, about the voyageurs and confederation and all that, but then we had Crooked River history lessons too. As far as I remember Crooked River history was just two stories and then a lot of stuff about railroads and mines and logging. Clarence arriving in his canoe and building his hotel was the first story, and Buddy Bryce finding the iron ore and them diverting the Crooked River and draining Red Rock Lake to get at it was the second one. George liked the first one best, probably for the same reasons he started getting *National Geographic* and going on expeditions and thinking of himself as a real explorer.

This is the story we heard in school.

On 6 May 1901, Clarence O'Callaghan paddled east up the Crooked River. Nobody was certain exactly where he started from. It might have been Fort Francis. It might have been anywhere. All they knew was that he must have paddled a long way – there were no roads here back then, not for hundreds and hundreds of miles. You travelled by water if you travelled at all, the same as the trappers and prospectors and loggers – who were the only white men who passed through these parts back then. Nobody saw much point in having roads in a place where it was all forest and water and swamp and bedrock. Nobody much planned on staying for long.

But they *were* planning to pass through it. That's what Clarence knew, that's what he was reckoning on. They were building a railroad to take wheat from out west to the port at Thunder Bay and then east down the St Lawrence into the Atlantic Ocean. And Clarence reckoned that the places where the trains would have to stop to refuel and re-water and whatever else those old trains had to do, well, there'd be men who had to stay put there. And they'd need somewhere to stay put. Clarence had an eye for an opportunity, our teacher told us. He took out a map, scratched his head, looked at where the railroad was being put through, flipped a coin or two, picked a spot, and started out in his canoe. He was sixteen years old. And he was right, too – about the spot. Right on the button. Two weeks after he set off the Canadian Northern Railroad announced they were putting in a division point – which was what they called the stopping places for trains – almost exactly where Clarence was headed. Except he didn't know that yet. There was nobody about to tell him as he made his lonesome way up the river.

And there was still nobody about when he arrived, not a soul. Picture this, our teacher would say, picture Clarence pulling his canoe up on the bank – near the very spot where the two old white pines grow – and looking around him. What would he have seen? Would he have seen the bank or Mike's Mart or the Red Rock Inn? Would he have seen the school we're sitting in? No. He would have seen those two white pines and behind them a whole bunch more white pines. There was nothing here back then, not a single building. So Clarence got out of his canoe, walked up the bank a couple of hundred yards, picked a piece of flat ground, and started building one.

When the railroad men arrived a few months later Clarence already had the foundations finished. 'What are you doing?' they asked.

'I'm building a hotel.'

'For who?'

'For you guys.'

'How'd you know we were putting a division point here?'

'I didn't.'

'Jesus H. Christ!' said the railroad men. 'I guess you're one lucky crazy son-of-a-bitch.'

Who knows why Clarence started building his hotel? Who knows why anybody does anything? That's what my nana used to say when crazy things happened, things you couldn't work out the reasons for. It sounded funny when she said it, in her accent. She must've heard it when she first came over and she spoke it like it was something special she'd found on her travels, like she'd kept all the new words and sayings she'd picked up in her new life as souvenirs. Who knows?

Our teacher, Mrs Arnold, was pretty sure she knew. She said it was because Clarence was a pioneering spirit. I don't think none of us kids knew exactly what that meant, only that pioneering spirits were restless and ambitious and had built Canada, the same as Mrs Arnold told us. But I couldn't quite get my head around that. I used to try imagining it, as if Clarence had woke up one day and thought, 'I'm feeling restless and ambitious today so I'm off to build Canada. First I'm going to have some breakfast, but right after that I'm off to build Canada.' What Virgil and Dad told me was that Clarence was the last of nine kids on a tobacco farm in Sarnia and he got sick of being the ninth and getting all the shitty jobs. They said one day, after cutting tobacco till the sun went down, he got into a fight with the eighth kid and got beaten. 'You're nothing,' said the eighth. 'You won't come to nothing. So you better keep cutting that tobacco and keep your trap shut while you're doing it.' The next day

Clarence was gone. One year later he was building his hotel. I couldn't work out why taking a beating would make someone start thinking about building Canada. Or a hotel. Or anything.

George didn't worry about all that stuff. He wasn't interested in the building part and everything that came after. The part he liked was the arriving bit, the one where Clarence was standing by himself in a place where nobody but Indians went, where each step took him onto ground he'd never seen before, onto ground hardly anyone had seen before. You could see George's face go funny even thinking about it. You could tell he was picturing himself there, stood wide-eyed in a world that was one big collection of exhibits, just waiting for him to find them.

Big Rock Candy Mountain

The week after we found the underground place George came over in the morning and told me he was going back there. I said I wasn't so sure that was a good idea, what with the chance there was a shacker living in it and everything, but George got in a huff and said he'd go anyway, with or without me, and I knew he'd not get far with just him paddling. OK, I said, and told him I'd go this one time and then we should leave it be. I don't like it there, I told him. He nodded his head and the brim of his hat slipped over his eyes.

'Why don't you wear a baseball cap like everyone else?' I asked.

'Why don't you shut up?' he said.

When we got to the riverbank we couldn't find the canoe anywhere. I had a look through the bulrushes and George tramped up and down through the bog-mat, poking around with this old walking stick thing he'd brought along. Well, that's that then, I said. *No* can do. Maybe if you'd look properly we'd find it, George said. But it wasn't there and no amount of looking was going to change that.

George huffed and puffed along the riverbank until his

pants were wet right up to his thighs. He got real ornery when he couldn't get started on his expeditions; it was what made his not being allowed out during the week so bad. Sometimes, when Mr McKenzie wouldn't let him go out into the woods, he'd kick the door until his toes were almost bleeding and then writhe and whirl about their garden like a mink in a trap, spinning and stewing in his own circle of tempers. If his face could've gone red it would've. Instead, tears would hang in the corners of his eyes and then fall onto his cheeks. His frustration had to boil up and go somewhere even if he wasn't allowed to.

Goddammit, he shouted, whacking a clump of innocent reeds with his stick. Goddammit. Goddammit.

Sitting there on the bank I was thinking there'd be no bulrushes left soon, when suddenly George calmed down.

'Of course,' he said to himself. 'Why didn't I think of that before?'

'Think of what?' I asked.

'It's elementary, my dear Eli.'

'It's what?' George had been reading detective books that winter and was always saying strange things out of them.

'Your grandfather's canoe. It's sitting right there in your garden shed. We can carry it here easy.'

'No way,' I said.

That was the last trip Clarence's canoe made before it became historical and ended up outside the museum. It wasn't hard to carry to the river because it was still made out of birch bark back then; the only hard part was getting it out of the garden shed with nobody seeing. At one point we dropped it on the road and just stood there glaring at each other. We were getting on each other's nerves I guess, because he wanted to go and I never did.

After we got out on the water George sat in the bow looking about as pleased as could be. He was thinking of himself being just like Clarence – or the Clarence he liked to imagine, at least – setting off into a brand new wilderness. You could tell he was thinking that because he kept jabbering on about our trip in the same style as Mrs Arnold had told us the story of Clarence's arrival. On 8 October George McKenzie paddled west down the Crooked River. Nobody was sure where he started out from . . . etc., etc. In the stern I was thinking about another Clarence: the one going around and around on the looping river and never getting anywhere.

It was harder to keep the birch-bark canoe straight than the other one, and what with George making his speeches the whole way instead of paddling properly it took us hours to get to the right spot, or near the right spot anyway. That's the thing with the bush around here – you'll reckon you know it, you'll reckon you'll easily recognize the places in it you've been before, but there's times it'll turn you around and you won't. That little creek you saw, that clump of spruces, that outcrop of rock, that piece of swamp, they'll go and change into a slightly different creek, a slightly different piece of swamp, a slightly different clump of spruces, and then you'll end up peering around you, and everything, for as far as you can see, will look like clumps of spruces and pieces of swamp and little creeks, all of them slightly different and all of them slightly the same. And then you'll feel it: the empty, scary space growing in your belly, growing bigger and bigger until it seems as big and empty as the thousands and thousands of kilometres surrounding you. And you'll feel the wildness of it then. And you'll know the fright that lives and breathes in that wildness too.

But we were lucky, if lucky is what you'd call it. As we rounded a bend George shouted back to me to pull over to the bank. I wasn't sure what he was up to, but when we got there he reached towards an overhanging spruce branch and grabbed hold of a piece of red tape wrapped around it. What's that? I asked him. I hadn't spotted it myself.

'It's a marker,' he said, as if I were an idiot for not knowing. 'You should always leave a marker.'

I'd never even seen him leave it.

As we got nearer the underground place I kept both my eyes on the ground. I had to. George's eyes were wandering excitedly all over the place. It was like he'd forgotten the bear trap and what it did to that sapling. And so he didn't see the signs I saw: the markers that weren't made of tape and weren't left on purpose.

I'd been out with Virgil when he hunted for moose and deer and seen him read the ground as easily and happily as he read his books. He'd see hoofprints and touch them with his finger and say that's from this morning or last night or last week; he'd see broken twigs or scrapings on the bark of trees or droppings and tell me whether it was a cow or a doe, a bull or a buck. Now, I saw a candy wrapper and knew it was a person. But when I tried to tell George he pretended not to hear me. He spent so much time looking for special things he didn't see the normal ones.

When we got inside the underground place, I couldn't stop staring at the open hatchway. I clung to the square of sunlight that fell through it like I was a minnow keeping close to cover, like down below was the dangerous shadow world – where the slubes hovered patiently on their slow-flickering fins – and up above was the safe place, the place you could hide.

George was busy picking through the stuff on the shelves. Every now and then he'd hold something up to me and say, hey Eli, look – a chisel, or a box of aspirin, or something like that. In the middle of the room he made a pile of the things he thought were the most interesting.

'If you take those you'll be stealing,' I told him.

'If nobody lives here it's salvage,' he said.

'Somebody lives here,' I said.

We'd been down there a half-hour or so when George moved over to the table with the map on it.

'I reckon whoever lived here travelled a lot and these circles are markers for all the places he went.'

'Like a hobo,' I said.

'Hobos don't have loads of stuff like this,' George said, as if he'd read about them in one of his *National Geographic*s and was a real expert on the matter. I wasn't no expert neither, but I remembered Nana talking about them and how they'd sometimes come on the boxcars in the summer and hang around town doing odd jobs. The ones who stayed a while became shackers. I remembered how Nana used to sing me one of their songs. It was about a place called Big Rock Candy Mountain, where cigarettes grew on trees and there were whiskey fountains. Sometimes she changed the cigarettes to candy canes and the whiskey to soda water but it didn't matter really – what mattered was it was a place where you could have pretty much everything you wanted. She told me they left markers too, secret ones on fences and doors, made of little circles and lines, to let other hobos know if the people who lived there were likely to give them food or jobs. I was going to tell George that, but he'd found a box of papers and books under the table and was rifling through them. He'd got about halfway through when an odd look came over his face. Holding a piece of paper up to the light of the flashlight he stared at the words on it like they were written in a language he'd half forgot and was trying to remember.

'What's it say?' I asked.

'It's not what it says,' he whispered. He wasn't sounding such an expert now, which kind of pleased me. 'It's . . . it's . . .'

And then the sunlight above me disappeared. It was like a cord or line or something had been cut and I felt like I was tumbling down into the shadow world where the slubes were waiting. Above me was the dark silhouette of a man.

'. . . it's *his* writing.'

*

'Hello, Mr McKenzie,' I said.

'Hello, Eli,' Mr McKenzie said. 'Hello, George.'

Mr McKenzie was staring down at us through the hatchway. There was no surprise on his face. He must have known someone was here; he must have seen the signs. His beard seemed huge, as red and huge as an Irish Santa's. Then his head disappeared and his boots started coming down the steps. Clump, clump, they went. Careful and steady. I saw George put the papers back and then glance nervously over at the pile of things on the floor. His mouth was half open and his skin was so white it was almost glowing.

'So,' Mr McKenzie said, 'I see you two have been doing some exploring.' He'd grabbed hold of the flashlight and was shining it into the corners. Its beam came to rest on George's pile. 'Or should I say stealing?'

'We didn't think anyone lived here, Dad,' George whimpered.

'Really, George. You didn't think that. But look around. It seems quite habitable here, doesn't it? More than quite. Very, I'd say. It looks very much like someone's made an extra-special effort to make it habitable, wouldn't you agree, Eli?'

I was going to say that I'd told George somebody lived here, but when I looked at Mr McKenzie I didn't say nothing. He was speaking in the way he used to in school: asking questions that he never expected you to answer, that he'd end up answering himself. But I was glad he was speaking like that and not like when he was speaking to

Mrs Arnold, telling her *this* and then telling her it again and again.

'Yes, I'd say someone had gone out of their way to make this a place they could live in – a place they could live in for a long time if need be.'

'But Dad,' said George. 'Nobody lives this far out of town, not even shackers.' The whimpering had gone out of his voice now, as if he'd remembered he was on an expedition and not at home.

'Perhaps that's the point of it, George. Had you even thought of that? Perhaps the reason for it being here is so no busybodies from town would poke their noses into it. Perhaps it's here because it wasn't *meant* to be found.' Mr McKenzie was talking to George but he was looking at me. I could see the sunlight from the hatchway where it tumbled onto the back of his head and lit up the fiery edges of his beard, but his face was in the shadows and I couldn't see his lips move. And again I got that feeling that time had got stretched or stuck down here. I felt like I was waiting for a school bell that might never ring. George shuffled from foot to foot and I knew he wanted to say something about what he'd found.

'Why is your writing on those pieces of paper?' he said at last.

'That,' said Mr McKenzie, 'is none of anybody's business.' His voice had gone quiet the same as when he'd told Mrs Arnold, 'This conversation is over.' And without even thinking I looked up at the rack with the deer rifle and shotguns. 'Now I think it's time we were all leaving, don't you?' George and I nodded and started walking towards the steps. When I'd almost got to the top of them he called up to me.

'Eli,' he asked, 'have you told anybody about finding this place?'

'No,' I said. 'I haven't told nobody.'

'Well,' he said. 'Why don't you keep it that way.' And when I looked back I could see his face coming into the light and his eyes were shining like the light was coming from inside them instead. I knew he wasn't asking me, then.

After we'd closed the hatchway we started walking back towards the river, Mr McKenzie first and then George and me. We'd got about halfway when Mr McKenzie stopped and turned around and said, 'I think it's best if George comes with me, don't you, Eli?'

They veered off upriver of where George and me had left Clarence's canoe, towards a thick cluster of bulrushes. George looked back at me for a second and then carried on behind his dad. He was keeping both his eyes on the ground now all right.

I didn't see George for a time after that. He wasn't even peeking out from behind the boards of the fence when I looked for him there. I bugged Gracie whenever I saw her, asking if George was coming out, but she just said his allergies were really bad and he couldn't for now. Gracie had started coming to our house quite a lot, ever since the summer when Mr McKenzie lost his job and started building the fence. She used to sit in the kitchen and talk to Nana and then to Virgil. Sometimes she'd be crying. She was different back in that time; I couldn't ever imagine her crying now. But already, even then, she seemed to be older than she really was.

Wolf Men and Circus Bears

After leaving Gracie and Mr Haney at the museum, I walked out towards where the tracks crossed the highway by the town sign. I was headed for the road to Eye Lake, but at the last minute I turned off towards the road to the old Red Rock mine site instead. I guess I was thinking things and wanted some peace and quiet, and these days there's nowhere more peaceful and quiet than the old mine site. There's nowhere more quiet than places that were loud once: it's a special kind of quiet, like the one in the basement of number one O'Callaghan Street.

I passed through the side of town where they'd built all the new houses for the mine workers – or at least they'd been new fifty years ago when they built them. Now they weren't in such good shape. Lots of them had lost their paint and boards and been patched up with insulation panels with the plastic wrapping still on them. Some hadn't been patched up at all and were tumbling down where they stood. There was broken-down machinery and upside-down boats and busted snowmobiles in most of the gardens, and dogs that'd turned as dirty and mean as dump cats. When I got to the Red Rock road I was glad.

It wasn't hardly ever used any more and there was fireweed growing high on the verges and a line of grass and bushes sprouting up along the middle. There used to be a trunk line connecting the mine to the main railroad and you could still just about follow it through the fireweed – the big wooden ties slowly splintering in the grass, the tracks turned orange-red with rust, and here and there the piles of iron ore pellets that'd spilled out of the rail cars once. The dirt on the road was almost the same orange-red as the rails and the pellets and the dust that still blew through town sometimes.

As you got closer to the site the road split, forking to the left and right, following where the shores of the lake used to be. On the right side, where the eastern shore used to be, you could see a kind of hollow in the land, meandering off into bush, where the Crooked River used to run. It was dotted with stunted jack pines and stones and piles of muddy gravel and sand from where they'd dumped the dredged silt from the bottom of the lake; there was a little stream running through it, which I didn't really remember being there before. To the left, where the western shore used to be, there was a great tear in the land, sheer and straight and full of huge, jagged boulders, where they'd blasted a rock cut and drained the lake's waters. There were pictures on the wall of our school, before and after ones, that showed what they'd done. In the 'before' one the Crooked River had flowed through the bush to the east and into Red Rock Lake, before flowing out of it and snaking and bending on its course through the middle of town. In the 'after' one there was a dam about two miles to the east and a big loop that went around through the bush to the north of Red Rock Lake, before joining the old course of the river again just before it reached town. This was the diversion. In the 'before' picture there was only green and a meandering ribbon of blue to the east. In the middle was a big patch of blue that said Red Rock Lake. In the 'after' picture there was a big patch of blue to the east and a big rusty red one in the middle. Red Rock Mine, it said on the red patch. Eye Lake, it said on the blue one.

I passed by where the mine buildings had been once; they were mostly gone but there were two still standing. They were made of corrugated iron and there were holes in them everywhere from where people used them for shooting practice. Beside them were wide, shallow pools of reddish water where not even a single bird sat on the surface or flew above. You couldn't feel a breeze or flutter of wind anywhere – it was like nature had stopped breathing or something, like its lungs were full of holes like everything else here was. And the biggest hole of all was Red Rock Lake.

I walked off the road where it forked, heading across to where the south shore had been. The ground was sandy here. It had been a beach once, before I was born. At its edge it fell away sharply into a great open pit.

All around the jagged edges of the pit you could see where the shore had been sandy or rocky once – it jutted in and out where the headlands and bays and fingers had been, and here and there islands stood up like pillars. Below them, on the pit's steep, sheer sides, were the layers that had been left, naked, when they took away the water. They went from grey-black to brown to orange to red, like some kind of giant knickerbocker glory. On the lake's old bed, bushes of balsam and poplar had started to grow since the trucks and diggers had stopped, and pools of water had settled around them. The pools and the churned earth were the colour of old blood, and looked deeper than I'd seen them before. Over to my right I could see a steady trickle of water tumbling over the edge of the pit.

I sat down on the sandy ground that used to be a beach and tried to do my thinking.

I was trying to think about what Gracie had said, about parts of me being like a fingerprint of Clarence and of parts of him being like a fingerprint of me. I figured it meant that wherever he was I was kind of there too. And if he wasn't the remains in the police station, if he was still going around and around in the Bermuda Triangle, then a piece of me was there with him, wherever *there* was. It was like there was a hole inside me too, one where bits of me kept falling into. And then I couldn't think about it any more and put my hands into the sand and started thinking about a picnic instead.

Sometimes, during summer evenings at number one O'Callaghan Street, one of the old-timers like Jim Clement or Jake Ottertale would drop by to have a glass of whiskey with Virgil before they went on to the Red Rock Inn. They'd sit out in the porch and talk, and sometimes, if that's where I was going to be sleeping that night, I'd get to stay up until they left. And so I'd listen as their voices murmured slow and mellow and husky against the hum of the mosquitoes beyond the screens and the trains gently creaking and shifting in their beds. They talked a lot about the old days, the days before the diversion and the mine, the days before Virgil even – when the Pioneer Hotel was still standing and Crooked River was still just a handful of railroad men and their families and the men working lumber. Sometimes they'd come over all wistful about it. But those days are gone, they'd say. And then they'd look sad for a second or two, as though they were surprised almost, as though they'd only just noticed they were. It was another world then, they'd say, but it's gone now. Yes, it's long, long gone.

Every summer back then in the long-gone days they'd have a picnic out on the south shore of Red Rock Lake – right where I was sitting, nearly. Pretty much the whole township went, as well as some of the Indian families who lived nearby. They'd set out first thing in the morning, carrying cobs of corn and guns and fishing rods, and when they got to the lake the women would dig pits in the sand and start fires and some of the men would head out in canoes to fish, while the others would go back into the woods to search for game to shoot. There was one picnic that was especially famous: the one where the wolf man and the circus guy came. It was Jim who told Virgil about that. Jim, with his quiet, chuckling smile and the thin red veins criss-crossing his nose. I missed him being about. He was part of my own long-gone days now.

The wolf man came from Minneapolis. He'd been in Crooked River for a week and was trying to kill wolves, except he wasn't using a gun or anything – he was using an axe and a suit made out of nails – and he wasn't having much luck. They've got a photo of him in the museum, with his suit on and his axe in his hands. The suit was made of leather and the nails were shoved through it so they stuck out all over like porcupine quills. Jim would get to chuckling whenever he mentioned him. Who knows what made him come here? he'd say. Who knows why people do what they do? The wolf man told everyone who'd listen that he was planning to make a living off all the pelts he was going to get, but he'd never even seen a wolf, Jim said, and he wasn't going to neither in that get-up. People had funny ideas about the north woods back then, he said. All sorts of funny ideas. Jim was just a boy himself and used to follow him into the woods and do wolf howls and make him run in circles through the bush holding his axe up ready, with sweat pouring down his face and mosquitoes buzzing around his head and his hands full of holes where he'd tried to swat them and hit the nails on his suit instead.

The circus guy arrived on a night train two days before the picnic. Jim said he'd seen him step out of the caboose, wearing a sharp suit and a hat, followed by a woman who was wearing a fur coat, even though it was summer. They walked together down the street to Clarence's hotel and Jim ran over to where the caboose man was leaning against his caboose, smoking a cigarette and waiting for the train to be loaded with coal and water.

'Where they from?' Jim asked. They weren't used to men in sharp suits getting off in Crooked River.

'From Chicago,' the caboose man replied.

'Is he a gangster?' Jim asked excitedly. The caboose man chuckled to himself.

'Well, sonny, if he's a gangster he ain't been too forth-coming about it. He says he owns a circus. But then again,' he said with a wink, 'he says that there woman is his sister, too.'

The first good look anybody got at them was the next day at lunch, in the dining room of the hotel. The man was still wearing his suit but the woman had changed out of her fur coat and was wearing a white silk blouse and a long black skirt and a black hat. There were pearls hanging from her ears, almost as white as her skin, and her lips were redder than any woman's in town. Usually all the people who stayed in the hotel sat together at one long wooden table for lunch and helped themselves from two big bowls that sat on either end of it. (Mostly it was rabbit stew, said Jim; Clarence used to pay him a few dollars a week to snare them.) But on that day Clarence had had a separate table set for the man and his sister. 'Because there's a lady present,' he informed the dining room when all of them at the long table saw the separate table. And he cooked a chicken for them too, said Jim – so he must have reckoned it was a real special occasion.

All through lunch Clarence made a fuss of them. He didn't have much in the hotel kitchen – just what would do for the rail and lumber men – but what he did have he brought out. Perhaps you'd like a few oranges for dessert, *he asked, and over at the long table the men's eyes popped out some. He sure kept them hid, a few of them mumbled.*

The man in the suit talked loudly all through his lunch, as if he were speaking to an audience. He told Clarence how they'd come from Europe with the circus as children, him and his sister. He hinted that they'd come from high-born blood but tragic circumstances had led to their father and mother's early death and they'd been cheated out of their inheritance. He stopped for a minute when he got to the part about the tragic circumstances and pulled a white handkerchief from his breast pocket and began dabbing his eyes with it. His sister put her hand across the table and clasped his. What a bucket of moonshine he was selling, Jim said. And nobody in the Pioneer Hotel was buying a drop of it.

Except my father, Virgil said.

I don't think he was buying into it either, Jim said. With respect to you and your mother, Virgil, I think it was her he was buying into. Or not even that. It was the idea of her – if you get my meaning right. Crooked River was a rough and ready place the wrong side of nowhere and we didn't get so many women visitors. And we got even fewer that wore silk and lipstick. Your father must've thought she was just about the finest lady who'd ever set foot in his hotel.

Why were they even here? Virgil asked.

Well, Jim said, when Clarence finally got around to asking the man replied they needed a bear – for their circus. The old one had died and they needed a cub, a living cub, to get trained and take its place. So how might

a man go about getting himself one of those in these parts?
the man asked, loudly enough for the whole room to hear.

'How much you willing to pay for it?' one of the rail-
road men at the long table asked.

'Fifty American dollars,' he said.

'You best come to the picnic tomorrow, then,' the man
told him.

The next morning they set off, most of the township,
on the narrow track that led to Red Rock Lake. Clarence
led the way, with the circus man and his sister on either
side of him. Then there was the Rooney family and
Mr Scheider, who owned the store; and Jake's mum
and dad and Joe Gordon, who was a trapper too; and
then . . . (Here, Jim would go through a bunch of names,
some of them that were still used in town and some that
weren't, nodding to himself as he went along, as if by
remembering them he was putting the whole long-gone
day of the picnic and that world back together, piece by
piece, person by person. And even though he never said
nothing about anyone going in any particular order, I
knew from the pictures and stuff in the museum they were
going Crooked River 1, 2, 3, 4 . . .)

I was lingering right at the back, Jim chuckled. The
wolf man had tagged along in his suit and Jake and some
of the Indian boys were sneaking through the bush on
either side of track, calling out to him like wolves. He
must've thought them woods was just full of them, he
chuckled.

When they got to the beach the women started digging out the fire-pits and some of the men set out in canoes to catch lake trout and walleyes, while the others went off to shoot partridge and whatever else they could find. Meanwhile, two of the railroad men, Jake's father, the wolf man, and two of the Indian boys stayed behind on the beach with Clarence and the circus man. His sister had sat herself down beneath an umbrella – a parasol she called it – and begun wrapping herself and her silk shirt in a plain cotton sheet. 'These flies,' she kept saying. 'These damn flies.'

'So what next?' asked the circus man.

'We're heading out to the blueberry patch,' Jake's dad said.

'What for?'

'For your bear.'

And so off they went – all of them except Clarence – towards the western shore where the best blueberry spots were. And why not Clarence as well? Virgil asked. With all due respect to you and your mother, Virgil, I think he had other things than bears on his mind, Jim winked.

When the others got to the blueberry patch it didn't take them long to find a she-bear and her cub. Now you stay back here, they told the circus man and the wolf man, and if she comes at you, you hotfoot it up one of these trees. Then the men crept closer and hid behind some bushes while the two Indian boys tracked around in the opposite direction, until they were on the other side of the bear and her cub. At a signal, the men and the Indian boys stood up suddenly and started hollering and beating the bushes with sticks. The bear and her cub ran this way and that in panic and the men and boys circled them, hollering and beating the bushes, until at last the she-bear would make a run at them and they'd split up and scatter into the woods. Soon enough she and her cub were separated, and then the Indian boys started calling out in the voice of the cub and drawing her further and further away into the bush, crying and bellowing and roaring for what she thought was her baby. The men came back and moved in a circle around the cub. When they caught it they tied up its limbs and snout with rope.

It all went like clockwork, Jim said. Except when they came back to the spot where they'd left the other two they found the wolf man stuck high up a poplar tree, trembling like one of its leaves. He lost heart with his hunting after that, Jim said. The day after the picnic Mr Gordon took pity on him and gave him two wolves he'd poisoned. They took a picture for him to take home, of him standing with his axe raised over one of the already dead wolves, and the day after that he was headed back to Minneapolis.

Back on the beach the fire-pits were ready and were heaped full of fish and game. And as they waited for it to cook, they sat down on the sand by the water and the children swam and the men drank from flasks of whiskey and smoked cigars and pipes and talked. The circus man was in full flow then, Jim said – stoked up with the whiskey and pleased with his bear – talking about his old country and the lost happy days of his and his sister's childhood.

*

They lived on the banks of the Danube, he told them, in a castle made of stone that shone almost white in the sun. It had columns and arched doors and a high tower topped with brightly coloured pennants that flapped merrily in the breeze. The gardens sloped down to the river's bank, dotted with great oaks and elms and beds of flowers and marble fountains where carved mermaids lounged beneath cascading founts of crystal water. Ah, those gardens, the man sighed, such a lush deep green they were, and so soft beneath my feet – like carpets. In the evenings he'd sneak out and watch the moon rise above the river, and it was such a big moon you'd feel as though you could reach out and touch it. (Ah, yes, Jim would sigh, there were moon-beams aplenty in that garden.) And the stars . . . they were stars like no others, like a thousand diamonds in the sky. And there were more diamonds in the castle too – on the nights when they had dances and balls in the main hall – shining from the tiaras and necklaces of the ladies as they waltzed beneath the lights of the chandeliers, the twirling satin of their dresses as sweet and soft as cotton candy. What enchanted nights they'd been, the circus man said. What a time and world it had been then! Marked by a glamour and beauty he'd never seen since.

We all sat and listened, Jim said. It was a pretty story. And what with the smells of the fish and game cooking in the pits and the mellow warm air of the afternoon, it was a pleasant enough picture to doze off into. The circus man seemed to be enjoying it as much as anybody and once he'd got into his stride I reckon he might've even half-believed it himself. The tear in his eye when he got to the tragic circumstances that'd taken it all away was almost real. Except this time there was no comforting hand offered by the sister. She sat through the whole perform-ance – wrapped in the sheet beneath the umbrella – without saying a word, not a single word. I reckon she'd heard it plenty of times already.

Clarence stood up then and, putting on his finest airs and graces, declared: 'If I might be so bold as to interrupt the gentleman, as everyone here knows we have a dance of our own here in Crooked River tonight and though we can't offer quite the finery and luxury of those dances he remembers, I hope we can at least offer our warmest hospitality.' And saying that he offered the sister an invi-tation he'd written in his very best hand on a small, white piece of paper.

Now the thing was, said Jim, we had those dances in Clarence's hotel every night after the picnics – and once a month through the whole summer too – but nobody had ever needed an invitation to go to them, let alone a written one. Everybody went. You just turned up and walked in the door. So you could see some of the wags from town smiling at this.

'Clarence,' one of them said. 'If I might be so bold as to interrupt, I must declare that I don't seem to have received my invitation as yet.'

'Well, I'll be damned if I haven't lost mine,' said another.

'Do they admit two, Clarence, or just the one?'

(Jim never said exactly what was written on that invitation, but I didn't ever need him to. It said: 'You

are cordially invited to the Crooked River Picnic Dance. I would be most honoured if you would attend. Yours, Clarence O'Callaghan. Proprietor.' I knew all this because it was right downstairs in the basement, in his trunk.)

That night at the dance Clarence played his fiddle, the same as he always did. Your father was the best in town, Jim said, which Virgil nodded at: he'd always said himself that Clarence was the best fiddler he'd ever heard. But that night he was real special, Jim told him. He did the jigs and reels, beating time on the floorboards with his boots, and his fingers were a blur and he never missed a note. He had them dancing so quick their heads were spinning and they hardly knew where their feet were. And then he'd switch to the slow sad Irish ballads and there'd barely be a dry eye in the place. And then back again to the fast stuff before those tears even had time to fall down their cheeks. He made that fiddle sing, Jim said – looking as though if he listened hard enough then he might still be able to hear it, like it might jump out of Clarence's trunk and start playing again – and every one of them songs was like the best you'd ever heard.

I don't know how long that dance went on for, Jim said, but it was longer than any of us remembered the other ones going on for. And that circus man, well, he was twirling and jumping and spinning with the best of them and he sure didn't look like no lord or sir then, like he was pining for those waltzes on the banks of the Danube. As for the sister, well she stayed sitting until almost the end of the night. Clarence was watching her as he played, and I reckon he was trying to tempt her up onto her feet the whole time, trying to play so good her feet wouldn't have no choice but to start moving. Until finally, right at the end, when the light was almost coming into the sky outside, she got up and walked to the floor. I'm not sure what Clarence was playing then – it wasn't one of his regular tunes – but there was a swing and a sway to it, a lilting this way and that, and when she started to dance she was moving just the same as it sounded. I'd never seen steps like that before; none of the women in Crooked River danced like that, and it was as if after a few moments you couldn't tell who was following who, whether she was following the notes or the notes were following her. There was a grace to it, a real grace, like a lily flower floating on a river's moving water; and watching her for a second you could almost believe in that castle and the moonbeams and the long green gardens going down to the banks of the Danube.

Yes, they were high old times, those times, Jim said. High times. I don't reckon hardly anyone in Crooked River was awake till noon the next day. I couldn't have slept more than an hour or two myself because I had to go check my snare lines and deliver the rabbits to the hotel kitchen. I remember walking through town with them – and when I say town I just mean O'Callaghan Street and the road that runs alongside the tracks, where the big roundhouse was where they'd park and fix the trains; there weren't any other roads in town then; there was hardly any town! – and it being so quiet you could hear the frogs chirruping down by the river and the horn of the eight o'clock train calling in the distance even though it was seven-thirty at most and it must still have been ten or fifteen miles off. And so I guess I was the only one who saw them leave – the circus man and his sister.

They were standing out front of the hotel. The man's suit wasn't looking half so sharp this time – it was crumpled and stained with whiskey and cigarette ash – and neither was he. His eyes were shot red and the oil in his hair had given up slicking it back and left it to fall over his forehead. Beside him was a wooden crate they'd put his bear cub in and you could hear it in there, whimpering and bellowing for its mother. But the man's sister, well, she looked just the same as when she'd arrived: in her smooth silk shirt and her hair done up in the back and shining like raven feathers and her lipstick making her lips redder than anyone else's in town. She was kind of hanging back from the man and the bear, as if she was waiting, and sure enough not five minutes had gone by when Clarence came on out the door of the hotel. He'd managed to get himself scrubbed up some and was wearing his black church suit.

'Please,' he said. 'If I can be of any assistance with your luggage?'

The eight o'clock train was getting louder now. It would've passed the narrows already.

'Well, I guess there's this here bear,' croaked the circus man.

'That's no problem,' Clarence said. And he must've spotted me then because he called out my name.

'Jim,' he said. 'Put them rabbits down and give us a hand with this bear, would you?'

So it was Clarence and me who ended up lugging that cub over to the platform. By the time we got it there you could hear the rumble and shake of the approaching train and the tracks were beginning to hum.

'It's been a great pleasure to make your acquaintance,' said Clarence, his voice raised against the noise.

'Yeh, yeh, and you,' replied the circus man, grimacing and clutching his forehead with one hand while he shook Clarence's with the other.

'If you're ever in these parts again you'd be most welcome. I can assure you I'd do everything in my power to make you happy here,' said Clarence, and he was looking sideways at her then.

'Why thank you,' she said. 'That's very kind of you.'

When they went to shake hands you never would have seen it if you weren't looking close: a piece of paper showing white against the pink of her palm, that was in his palm then, and went straight into his pocket. It happened in less than a blink of an eye, but I was sure I recognized that piece of paper – it was the invitation he'd given her on the beach. And then the train had arrived and in all the steam and commotion I hardly noticed them climb up into the red caboose.

Clarence and me waited on the platform for the train to pull off again. It started slow and as it picked up speed, I kind of got the idea he didn't want me there and I began to skulk back towards where I'd left the rabbits. I'd only gone fifty yards or so when the train rounded the

curve in the tracks and snaked into the green of the bush.
And as the red of the caboose disappeared I heard it, as
plain as day: a sort of short, anguished bellow coming
from Clarence's lips. He sounded just like the mother bear.

That was how Jim told the story of the famous picnic, one
night as he and Virgil sat on the porch and I lay there,
listening. I think Virgil wanted him to stay: he'd sure
poured him plenty of whiskey as he'd been talking. But
then Nana came to the door into the porch and said I had
to get my sleep and if they wanted to carry on jawing
they'd have to take it over to the Red Rock Inn.

'We'll have to finish this conversation another time,
Jim,' Virgil said.

'Sure thing,' said Jim.

And then Jim walked out into the dark humming night.
He'd only taken a few steps before Virgil called out to him
through the screen windows.

'How soon after that did he start on his castle, Jim?'

'Pretty soon. The next week or so, I reckon. But I
couldn't be sure on that front, Virgil – he didn't announce
it or nothing and we never even knew what he was up to
properly for about a year.'

'Thank you, Jim. We'll continue this another time.
Soon.'

'Any time,' said Jim, and there was just his voice
coming from the darkness. 'Any time you like, Virgil.'

After his footsteps had gone Virgil stayed on the porch
a while, staring out into the night. Then he finished off his

glass of whiskey and said goodnight and left me alone on the porch, listening to the chirruping of the frogs and the thrumming of the crickets, sounding like steel cables pulled too tight. For a while I couldn't close my eyes because every time I did I'd see Clarence there, going around and around and around on the looping river until it made my head hurt – thinking of the forever of it. But then at last he was gone and I laid my head down on the couch and waited for the night trains to sing me loudly to sleep.

And I wished they still could've sung me to sleep, like they used to. Because when I looked down over the edge of the beach, which had become a cliff now, lapped by thin air, I could feel my circle of tempers beginning to turn again, and their faces and voices – Virgil's, Jim's, Nana's, all of them – were spinning around in my head like a whirlpool, as if someone had pulled a plug in the bottom of the empty lake and they were being sucked down into it like water, like the water that was already gone.

The End of the World

The next time I saw George it was Halloween. At first I didn't think I would. Usually on Halloween he'd come over early in the morning and stalk around our kitchen, talking about his plans: what houses we should go to, which people would have the most candy, what route to take – that kind of stuff. But when I got up and looked out the window there was nobody about. Across the road the McKenzies' fence stood tall and silent and there was no face between the thin gaps in the boards. Pressing my fingers against the glass I could feel the sharp, almost hurtful, cold of a frost outside and realized the trees were all coated in white.

The smell of warm sugar was drifting up from the kitchen and when I went downstairs I found Nana pouring hot syrup out of a pot onto a baking tray. She was shaping it into fish and moose and bears and other, stranger, creatures I didn't recognize for certain: witches and goblins, things like that, from her old country. When I was younger she'd told me stories about them but I never remembered the stories properly – except one about a giant slube who ate the whole world.

'My little one,' she said, turning around as I walked into the kitchen. 'Would you like to taste?'

She offered me a spoonful of the warm syrup. It was sweet and delicious. Strands of it dripped down onto my chin. Then she carried on shaping it into her strange creatures and put them on a windowsill to cool and harden. This was the candy the trick-or-treaters got at number one O'Callaghan Street.

After a while I decided I'd go over and try to find George. Virgil and Dad had both told me to stay away from there for a while, but I was worried I'd have to spend the whole of Halloween just with Billy if George didn't come out. Outside in the garden I found the rainwater had frozen in the bucket I kept frogs and toads in during the summer. We used to hunt for them back then; the frogs in the daytime and the toads at night, with flashlights. I never knew where they went in the fall and winter. Mrs Arnold said in school that some animals were warm-blooded and others cold-blooded but what difference that made was a mystery to me and it still never explained where the frogs and toads went. I always pictured them in some hidden place – a cave or a deep tunnel under the ground, with long icicles hanging from the ceiling – huge piles of frogs and toads, their bodies frozen stiff in sleep and frosted white, their skin as crystal-smooth as Nana's candy animals, and inside their guts and veins turned into a solid, icy tangle. And when I got to George's house and saw the curtains on his window closed I suddenly pictured him inside, freezing and curled up asleep – the same as the hidden frogs and toads. I was going to throw a stone at his window then, to wake him, but I could hear shouting coming from behind the fence and so turned back.

Outside the gate to our garden a ball of ice hit me on the side of my head and I turned around to find Billy grinning at me from the sidewalk. He'd been scraping the frozen surface of a puddle with a shovel.

'This is even better than snow,' he said.

'That really hurt,' I told him.

'Don't be such a baby,' he crowed. 'Baaa baaa, Eli the baby. Come on. My mum says you should come over.'

'I have to help my nana making candy,' I told him.

'No, you don't. I just been at yours and she says it's fine.'

Over at the Bryces' place they were going through huge mountains of candy that Buddy must have had delivered from Thunder Bay. Brenda was at the table sorting out mixtures of them and putting them into pink paper bags. There were chocolate drops, pieces of red liquorice, wine gums . . . everything you could think of.

'Well hello there, Eli,' she said smiling. Brenda was always smiling. Whatever anyone said or did she would always smile.

'The same of each, Brenda, the same of each . . .' whistled Buddy, who was sitting at the head of the table beaming, looking pleased with himself like he was the King of Big Rock Candy Mountain. 'The same for everyone.'

Not that it *was* going to be the same for everyone. Out of the corner of my eye I could see Billy grabbing handfuls of candy out of the bags and stuffing them into his cheeks and pockets. When Brenda saw him she just smiled. 'Now, Billy, there's no need for that, is there? There's plenty to go around.' Billy carried on as if he'd not heard her.

'Now then, Eli, would you like to try some of these?' Brenda asked me, lifting a few chocolate drops off the mountain. She always spoke real slow to me. And she always sounded sorry for me too, as if I'd just had a puppy die or something.

'So, what are you dressing as tonight, then?' Buddy asked from the head of the table.

'Spiderman.'

'Spiderman!' Billy spluttered. Some of the liquorice he'd stuffed into his cheeks came flying out onto the table and lay there half-chewed. '*Spiderman*,' he repeated with a shake of his head. 'That's so crappy.'

'Billy, you shouldn't say things like that to Eli,' Brenda said with a smile.

'But it's true, Mum. Spiderman is *so* crappy.'

'It's an interesting choice, Eli – an interesting choice, certainly,' Buddy said. 'Billy's going to be a pirate.' He said this proudly, as if he were saying prime minister or astronaut or something.

Later on Billy let me know that he had all sorts of plans for the evening, most of which involved throwing eggs at people's houses. He showed me a bag he'd stolen out of the fridge and stashed under his bed. He said he was going to go as far as Eye Lake to throw them at the shackers' places. I said I didn't want to go. I didn't even like think- ing about Eye Lake at night back then, especially near the shackers' places. Except I couldn't tell Billy that. 'Suit yourself,' he said. '*Scaredyman!*'

I don't remember exactly where I spent the rest of that day – maybe I was at the baseball diamond or the gravel pit – only that I must've been outside because I remember watching flocks of geese go by above me in their swaying Vs. Their honking sounded sad and lonely somehow. It was an end-of-fall sound, the sound of everything leaving us behind for the winter. Above the geese, clouds had starting drifting across the sky: thick, low-hanging, yellowy-grey clouds. And then the air beneath them went real still and the wood smoke rose up in straight lines from the chimneys until its grey seemed to bulge and spread against the surface of some invisible barrier and mix into the yellowy-grey of the clouds. The sky felt closer, heavier, like a giant lid being placed down on us from above. The first snow of the year began to fall as the last light of the day began to fail.

By then I was back at O'Callaghan Street, because I remember watching the flakes land against the kitchen windows and slide down the glass as Nana fussed over my costume. The top was fine – it was from the Marvel company and Dad had let me sign the order form in my own shaky letters – and so was the mask; it covered your whole head and neck and had a round hole at the front for your eyes and nose, like a balaclava. The problem was the bottoms. When I'd put them on they'd ripped at the back and Nana was trying to put a few stitches in to hold the rip together until she could fix it properly. It would have been an easy job, except that I was refusing to take them off. I don't know why I was being such a pain in the neck – Spiderman was always good to his nana. I started blubbering every time she tried to pull the bottoms down.

There was a knock at the door then and I was dreading it being Billy and him seeing me blubbering and spotting the hole in my pants and saying how crappy Spiderman was. But it wasn't Billy. It was George. He was wearing an old deerstalker hat and a tweed jacket and pants. 'I'm a detective,' he told me and Nana.

'Don't you look nice,' Nana said.

Virgil poked his head into the kitchen from the living room, where he was listening to his records. 'I thought I recognized that voice,' he said, sounding a bit surprised. He looked at George.

'Sherlock Holmes,' he said.

George smiled.

Before we headed out trick-or-treating Nana made me put on a pair of snow pants and a jacket, so the hole didn't matter any more.

Out in the garden I saw that a thin layer of snow had already settled on top of the ice in my frog bucket. I asked George where he'd been earlier.

'My dad said I was too allergic to go out,' he said. 'But then my mum said I was fine to go out, especially on Halloween. They had a big discussion about it. My dad said I could go out for a bit.'

We didn't get more than a few yards down the sidewalk before Billy appeared. He was wearing an eyepatch and a bright red scarf. There was a big golden hoop hanging from his ear. He looked George up and down and was going to say something but he didn't. Instead he told George about his plans to go out to Eye Lake and throw eggs at the shackers' places. George hadn't been any-where for almost a month. I knew he was going to say yes and I knew I'd have to go then.

We took the street behind Main. The only cars on it were old, broken-down ones, parked up at the backs of the out-of-business stores. In the gaps between the stores, across the empty lots, we caught glimpses of other groups of trick-or-treaters, making their way in straggles up Main beneath the street lights. Here and there one of the lights would be broken and they'd disappear into the shadows and the falling snow. We went past the museum and the school until we reached where the train tracks curved away into the woods. There were piles of old railroad sleepers heaped higgledy-piggledy on the verges and the settling snow gave them strange shapes, like Nana's candy creatures. After passing the town sign, we slipped onto the dirt road to Eye Lake and the lights of the town vanished straight away as though they'd never been there in the first place. It was almost completely dark now and none of us spoke. Beneath our feet the road was frozen solid and the only sound was the occasional crunch when one of our boots shattered the ice of a puddle – but even this was muffled by the falling snow.

After a while my eyes got a bit more used to the dark and I could make out the pines and spruces looming up above me on either side, a deeper black against the blackness of the cloudy night. And then eventually the black edges began to thin and one big patch of darkness opened up in front of us. We'd reached Eye Lake.

Billy had hung back behind us on the road, but as soon as we reached the boat launch he shoved ahead to the front and we followed him along the strand of sand on the shore. There was a crust of ice beginning to form at the edges of the lake and the snow was settling on top of it. I was glad of that. I thought maybe the watchers wouldn't be able to see us now: that the ice and snow was like a lid that closed their eyes.

And then at last we made it to the Earl's shack.

You could only see it at first because of the thin slivers of light that leaked through the drawn curtains of the windows. But slowly the shape of the cabin itself became visible: a squat ugly shadow, cowering in the dark like one of the toads we hunted for at night in the summer. Billy placed himself carefully behind the low hanging branches of a pine tree and opened his bag of eggs. He gave George and me two each.

'Aim for the windows,' he whispered. He sounded horribly gleeful.

Billy threw first, and then me and George together. I guess one or two of them must have hit because before long the door latch clicked open. We crouched further down behind the branches and watched. A line of light fell out of the door onto the ground in front of the cabin, which was covered in a dusting of snow.

'Who's there?' came the Earl's voice from behind the door. 'Who is that?' His accent seemed out of place out there in the night, in the falling snow, like some strange twittering bird blown off its course into the wrong place.

The line of light began to grow, widening out from the opening door into a triangle that spread just to the side of us on the snow. At its source, standing under the door frame, was the Earl, dressed in a tweed woollen suit like George's. He was wearing his glasses, the ones with the small thick circles for lenses. He took several steps forward and stood there in the snow, flailing with his hands at the flakes in front of his face as if they were a swarm of mosquitoes.

'I know you're there,' he called out. 'I know perfectly well that you're there.'

George started to shuffle backwards, towards the lake, but Billy and me stayed put. I think he knew the Earl wouldn't be able to catch us. And I already knew for certain he wouldn't. I remembered the first time I'd seen him, when he'd stood with his arms spread out before him and said about this being his Bermuda Triangle. I hadn't really understood what he meant back then but now here it was, the triangle, drawn on the ground in front of him. He could walk to its edges but he couldn't pass beyond them.

Billy threw another egg. It landed just inside the open door.

'Your parents will find out about this. I can assure you of that.'

The next one hit the door jamb.

'Look,' said the Earl, 'will you please just leave me be?'

He was standing right at the boundary of the light and

we could see the two small discs of his lenses glimmering in front of his eyes. There were droplets of water on them from where the snowflakes had melted.

'Come on,' I whispered to Billy. 'That's enough. Let's leave him be.'

The next one hit him plum on the forehead. Some of the yolk stuck to the thinning bangs of his hair while the rest slid down over his nose and glasses. He made a half-hearted attempt to wipe it off with his sleeve but that only smeared it and in the end he turned sadly around and walked back towards the door. The triangle of light disappeared as he closed it behind him. I could feel something wet dripping over the cuff of my mitten onto my wrist and it was only then I realized that I'd crushed my second egg in my hand.

'Let's leave him be,' I said.

Billy wanted to go on to the next cabin, further along the shore, but I'd had enough. I never wanted to throw another egg as long as I lived. George was standing by the lake rooting around in the piles of driftwood there, and when Billy told him his plans I thought he'd want to go too, just to see what was there, just to explore. But he said he couldn't. He said he wasn't allowed out late because of his allergies. Billy got in a big huff.

'My dad says you're not allergic to anything,' Billy said. 'He says your dad's gone nuts.'

George tried to hit him but Billy just laughed and pushed him onto the driftwood. I wanted to hit Billy as well then, except he was already walking away along the shore with his bag of eggs.

'You two are a real pair of loons,' he shouted back at us. 'Loooooooons,' he shouted, trying to sound like one.

George didn't say anything until we were halfway back to town. Usually he'd be telling me stuff all the time or doing his *National Geographic* speeches or something, but now he was quiet, as though the snow was muffling him.

'He's not nuts,' he said at last. 'He's not.'

We were almost at the town sign before he spoke again. The snow was falling heavier and heavier. Under its whiteness Crooked River looked different – like a new place, like another town. It always did after the first snow. And then we'd get used to it and it'd look like the same old town again.

'It's just he knows stuff, stuff other people in town don't know. He says he's done all the research and he says at least we'll be prepared, even if nobody else is. He says that's why he made our fence so high – so he could prepare things without everybody else knowing.'

'What stuff?' I asked.

'About what's happening everywhere, about how it's all going to turn out.'

'How what's going to turn out?'

'The world,' George said.

And that's when he told me about the end of the world.

Of course his dad couldn't say exactly what day it would happen. That would've been impossible, George said. But with the current situation it was definitely going to happen. It's imminent, George said – which meant soon, he told me. Then he started talking about nuclear missiles and pre-emptive strikes and Ronald Reagan and the Russians. He said his dad had calculated which cities in North America would be hit and how far the destruction would spread and how long the fallout would last. Fallout was radio-active, which meant it was poisonous, and it would fall just the same as the snow was falling. George was telling me all this at a hundred miles an hour, as if he'd been storing it up the whole month, and I knew it wasn't really him talking but Mr McKenzie: it was the same as when he made his *National Geographic* speeches.

None of it made much sense to me. I'd heard some of those things on TV but that was far away and this was Crooked River. The news didn't happen in Crooked River. In the *Crooked River Progress* there was a section called 'Police Watch', which was Virgil's favourite section. He read it out whenever he got a new edition. His favourite one ever was about a dog. *12.58 p.m.*, it went. *Dead dog spotted lying in the centre of Main Street. Plans made for its removal. 12.59 p.m. Dog moved on of own volition.* I reckoned it was a good bet the end of the world wouldn't happen here.

As we passed the museum I asked George what his mum thought about the end of the world.

'Mum doesn't know the details,' he said. 'Dad says she doesn't need to know them yet. She'd only get worried. He only told me because we found the underground place.

The underground place is where we're going to live when it happens.'

I didn't say nothing for a bit then and George started to twitch and look nervous. He took off his deerstalker hat and the snowflakes fell onto his hair, which was so white you could hardly see them there.

'You can't tell anybody,' he blurted out. 'I wasn't supposed to tell anybody. Dad says when it happens the people who haven't prepared will try taking all our things. That's why nobody can know where the underground place is, even Mum.'

We were almost back at number one O'Callaghan Street by then, and when we got to the gate into the garden we stopped and stood there for a while. Normally George would've come in with me for a cup of cocoa but he hung back now, shifting from foot to foot like he had something more to tell me.

'Maybe he'll let you stay with us, Eli. I could ask him.'

I thought about that for a second.

'What about Nana?' I asked. 'And Virgil and Dad?'

He didn't say nothing then. There was a tight feeling in my chest and a burning feeling at the back of my head. I was too mad to say anything so I turned around and left him and walked through the gate on my own.

That night I slept in my Spiderman suit. I hoped it'd protect me from the bad thoughts that kept creeping into my head. Whenever I closed my eyes I could see the Earl's face, covered in egg, staring out at me from the triangle. And then the watchers. They could see me past the edges of the ice and their heads were swaying back and forth unhappily on the lake's bed. The snow was falling, except instead of settling it was melting everything. The Earl's face was going bit by bit, until there was only his glasses left hanging in the air where his face should have been. And then I realized that the watchers were Virgil and Nana and Dad and Clarence, and the snow was falling clean through the water and landing on their faces too and bit by bit they were melting until there was nothing there but the empty bed of the lake. And then I must have fallen into sleep, because the next thing I remember is hearing the sound of Virgil's truck clunking and clattering through the icy potholes of O'Callaghan Street. I was so relieved I jumped straight out of bed and ran down into the kitchen in my Spiderman suit. Nana was leaning over the sink but I was past her and through the door before she had the chance to tell me to put my coat on. Outside the sky was clear and the sun glistened over the surface of the new white snow.

Prairie Flowers

'Are you going to the birthday party?' Bobby asked.

I was sitting out front of the Tamarack dorm, sorting through my tackle box. They've got a curious way of getting all tangled up, do tackle boxes, however careful you are putting stuff back into them. But I've always enjoyed sorting through them. It's real soothing somehow – finding the right place for everything and discovering old hooks and lures you don't even remember having. I'd already found one of Virgil's old ones in the bottom of my box: a home-made jig, with black eyes and bright red and yellow feathers, like some kind of south sea idol.

'Whose party?'

Bobby looked at me as if maybe I was joking him. But I wasn't.

'Crooked River's!' he said. 'You must know about *that* birthday. We've been doing stuff in school for it all week and there's posters and everything all over town.'

'I knew about the birthday. I guess I must've forgot about the party.'

And I had clean forgot. The day before, as I was walking back from the mine site, a car had pulled up beside me and it was Officer Red, who was called that because his hair was that colour, almost the same colour as the dust on the road.

'Hey there, Eli,' he'd called out from the window of his car. 'This is some coincidence – I was just meaning to call on you out at the Poplars.'

I reckon it was a coincidence. He did a lot of driving, did Officer Red. Because there was less and less people in Crooked River there was less crime too and so he just drove around a lot hoping someone might break a law or two.

'Where you been?' he asked.

'Out at the mine site,' I said. 'I was on the beach, where they used to have the picnics.'

'Beaches and picnics, eh? I don't recall ever seeing either of those on the mine site. You weren't shooting up those buildings?' he asked. 'Because I've sure noticed a bunch of holes in them.'

'I wasn't shooting nothing,' I said.

He smiled then and said, 'I was only kidding, Eli. Now, why don't you hop in the car and we can go down the station?'

In the station house everyone had seemed pretty excited. Sergeant Hughie was pointing this way and that and Miss Kadychuk the secretary was scurrying around trying to follow his pointing. There was a man I hadn't seen before, standing by the desk, and I think all the fussing and pointing was to find him a room to use. I guess I'd come in sooner than they'd expected. As I watched them I remembered Virgil reading out the Police Watch.

12.58. Dog in road. 12.59. Dog departed of its own volition. Sergeant Hughie waved to me and Officer Red told me to take a seat.

'Don't you worry yourself, Eli. This is all just routine,' he told me, looking kind of proud and important as if this much was always happening in the station.

It was the same as what Gracie had said. They wanted to get a sample from me, of my DNA stuff. I didn't know what they needed for a sample.

After they'd sorted out the room for the man, Officer Red led me over to the door and we went in together.

'This is Officer Mathieu,' Officer Red said. 'He's from forensics in Thunder Bay and he'll take your sample.'

'It's very simple, Mr O'Callaghan,' said Officer Mathieu. 'All we require is a single swab with some of your saliva on it.'

A swab. I looked at him and then at Officer Red.

'It's that,' Officer Red told me, pointing at Officer Mathieu's hand. He was holding one of them things you clean your ears with. He put it in my mouth for a second and that was that. Apparently even a tiny drop of my spit had a fingerprint of Clarence in it. Even my spit was full of bits of lost people.

Afterwards Officer Red told me it wouldn't take them long to get the results, and as he was leading me to the door out he started asking if I was going to the street party they were having to celebrate the township's birthday. 'But of course you will be,' he'd said, answering his own question. 'You being related to the founding father and all that.' And then he'd looked over at some plastic bags with tags on them that were sitting on a desk in the corner and stopped speaking, as if it weren't proper to bring Clarence up when it might be his remains right there in those bags. But I wasn't thinking about those remains. I was thinking that if I spat on the ground there'd be bits of them all in it somehow.

'So,' Bobby asked, 'are you going?'

'I'm not too sure,' I said. 'I don't feel much like celebrating, Bobby.'

'But there's going to be a parade and floats and everything. My teacher said there's even going to be a float with someone dressed up as your grandfather on it.'

'I'm not so sure,' I said.

'Please,' Bobby said. 'My mum doesn't want to go – because of the bruises on her face. But she might go if you go, and if she doesn't then I could go with you.'

I said yes then, even though I didn't want to go. It seemed like I always ended up going places I didn't want to go.

The three of us walked together down the dirt road towards town. The sun was out and it was warm and the smell of the pine sap was soft and sweet. It was already hard to even imagine there'd been a winter. It was like this every year – the seasons slipped from one to the other so fast it was like you'd just blinked and didn't quite believe what'd been in front of your eyes the second before. Bobby was scouting through the verges for frogs and toads. I would've liked to have joined him. When he was around it made me want to do all the stuff I used to do when I was a kid.

Sarah was wearing a dress with pictures of flowers on it. She looked really pretty, even with her black eyes. She was wearing sandals too but after a bit she slipped them off and started walking in her bare feet.

'I love being able to walk barefoot,' she said. 'It's amazing, isn't it? It seems like yesterday it was winter and now you'd never even believe it. Thank you so much for coming with us, Eli. I haven't felt much like going anywhere recently.'

I was happy then, thinking how we'd been thinking the same thing. And then I wanted to ask her where all the frogs and toads went in the winter, because I'd been thinking that as well when I was watching Bobby.

When we came to the crossing I looked down the rail tracks and there were flowers growing everywhere at the sides, beyond the cinders. There were pink ones and delicate blue ones and yellow ones. I'd never known their names and they only ever grew by the sides of the tracks. Virgil told me they were prairie flowers and grew from seeds that fell off the grain trucks when the wheat trains passed through. I remembered watching them passing – the trucks coloured half yellow and half rusty brown, with a big picture of a head of wheat on each one – and how many there seemed to be. They'd go on and on until it seemed like the train was a hundred miles long, so long you could imagine how big and wide the prairies were just from watching them go past. And looking at the flowers now I wondered if Sarah recognized them and knew their names from when she lived out west, and if she'd seen the fields of wheat that'd filled all those trucks. I was going to ask her that, but before I could she'd taken hold of my hand and was holding it in hers. Her skin felt as soft and smooth as pine sap.

Outside the museum doors Mr Haney was standing on a platform made of boards, dressed as a voyageur. He had a buckskin coat on, with tassels on the front, and a red scarf and hat.

'Ça va,' he called out to us as we walked by. He was smiling and happy. There were a bunch of people outside the museum, as many as the town could muster.

Beside Clarence's canoe there was a table where they were giving out hotdogs, and a barrel full of corncobs, and another table where a big cake sat with a hundred candles on it. Mrs Hamalainen and Mrs McKay were handing out the food and Mrs Arnold was standing nearby talking to Gracie. She didn't teach any more – she'd retired. Her hair was grey all over these days.

'Hi there, Eli. Good to see you here,' she said. I tried to remember something she'd taught us in school, so I could show her I'd remembered it, but I couldn't think of nothing.

'Hello, Mrs Arnold,' I said.

'Please, Eli. I think you can call me Frances now. And who is this?' she asked, smiling down at Bobby.

'This is Bobby,' I said. 'And this is . . .'

'Hello, Sarah,' Mrs Arnold said. 'I'm so glad you could make it.'

Everyone has always met everyone else in Crooked River. I forget that sometimes.

Mrs Hamalainen and Mrs McKay were busy shoving hotdogs and corn and pieces of cake into Bobby's hands. They were cooing over him and mussing his hair and he looked a bit nervous. It was like all the grown-ups were searching out kids to give stuff to – like there weren't enough to go round.

'If I were you I'd get some hotdogs down you quick and get going before Tom there starts off with his speeches,' Gracie whispered to me. 'I swear he spent three hours practising them yesterday – maybe more. I was asleep after ten minutes.'

But it was already too late for that. Buddy Bryce, the Reeve, and a few other old-timers had sat down on chairs on the platform, and Mr Haney had rounded up some kids to stand in front of it and sing 'O Canada'. A couple of them were dressed as voyageurs as well, but most of them weren't. As soon as they'd finished he stepped onto the platform himself and started fussing with a microphone.

'Jesus,' Gracie rasped. 'He doesn't need that damn microphone. We're hardly the five thousand here, are we?'

'Testing. Testing, one, two, three,' Mr Haney said into the microphone, but you could only hear his normal voice.

'Everyone can hear you just fine as it is, Tom,' someone shouted.

'Get on with it,' Gracie called up at him.

'It's a great pleasure,' he began, 'to see so much of our community gathered here today to celebrate a hundred years of Crooked River. What an achievement it's been. For a community like ours to grow and flourish in the wilderness has been no mean feat. Of course over those hundred years there have been ups and downs and obstacles to overcome, but each time, pulling together as a community, we've managed to overcome them. I'd say Crooked River truly is "The Little Town Who Could".'

Mr Haney went on for quite a while after that, talking about Clarence and the railroad and the mine and just about everything that'd happened in Crooked River over the last hundred years – at almost the same speed it'd happened too, it felt like. One of the old-timers fell asleep on his chair. Then Buddy made a loud coughing noise and Mr Haney said: 'But to conclude, I'd like to make a special presentation to one of our citizens for their exceptional contribution to the life and history of our community. The story of Red Rock Mine belongs not only to our town's history, but goes down as one of the most audacious and remarkable feats of industry and engineering in the history of our entire nation. That story began with one man and his vision. While others before him had suspected that somewhere beneath our wilderness lay a potential wealth of iron ore, it had eluded all of them; until one day a young man arrived in this town with nothing more than a hunch, a bagful of determination, and an unshakeable ambition to succeed. Where others had confined themselves to the probable – to the shore, if I might put it that way – he let his vision range further, across the water.

Where they saw a lake, an insurmountable obstacle, he saw a possibility. And so it was, almost sixty years ago now, that he walked out onto the ice of Red Rock Lake, drilled down through it, and discovered the ore lodes beneath its bed. And of course that was only the beginning. I'm sure all of us here know the subsequent history: how, as the president of Red Rock Mines, this man assembled the finest, most imaginative engineers and undertook nothing less than the diversion of a whole river and the draining of a whole lake; how he brought out the first loads of ore; how – sixty years ago – he turned a small railroad division point into a thriving and prosperous town. As a token of the township of Crooked River's gratitude for all his many achievements, I would now like to present a special "Outstanding Living Citizen" award to Buddy Bryce. I'm sure he'll be the first to appreciate the material out of which it's been constructed.'

At that Mr Haney handed Buddy a big key made out of iron. It must have been pretty heavy because you could see him stoop when he took hold of it. Maybe he didn't appreciate that so much. Most of us thought he was going to drop it, and the crowd kind of held their breath. Then, with a grimace, he managed to lift it up for a second before putting it down on his chair and the people all clapped. I could see Brenda right at the front by the platform with the biggest smile on her face I'd ever seen, but I couldn't see Billy anywhere. Buddy turned to face them then, beaming through his wrinkles like I remembered him beaming at the table in front of the Halloween candy all those years ago, like he was the King of Big Rock Candy Mountain.

After the presentation there was a parade organized for Main Street and everyone began drifting over there. Sarah, Bobby and me drifted with them for a bit, but then, out of the corner of my eye, I saw Billy sitting in his truck in the museum parking lot, drinking a bottle of beer and staring right at us.

'I reckon it'd be nice to go the other way,' I told Sarah and Bobby. 'Down along the river. They won't be starting the parade for a bit.'

'That a great idea, Eli,' Sarah said. I reckoned she'd seen Billy too.

When we got to the river I noticed straight away how low it was. This early in the summer the water should have been a lot higher. I stopped by the old railroad bridge, where the trunk line had gone across to the mine site, and looked down at the pools behind the iron pylons where George and me used to fish with red and white bobbers. They were hardly deep enough to fish in now, and the current was so weak it wouldn't have even shifted a bobber.

'What you looking at?' Bobby asked.

'Just an old fishing spot,' I said.

'What did you used to catch there?'

'Just slubes, mostly. And walleyes too, sometimes – early on after the ice melted in the spring, when they're moving after spawning.'

'What's spawning?'

'That's them making more fish,' I said.

Sarah sat behind us on the grass, staring at the river with her black eyes. Bobby walked up and down the bank a bit, looking into the water trying to see if he could spot fish between the thin weeds that moved this way and that in the current like long human hair, the same as I used to do when I was a kid. But I doubted there were many down there: all the cover for them was stranded out in the air because the water was so low.

They'd made a real effort with Main Street, as much as they could do. There was bunting hanging off most of the storefronts, even the ones that were just fronts and nothing else, and a big 'happy birthday' sign hanging across the street. It was cheerful and bright as long as you didn't look too close, or sideways – onto the empty lots with the weeds and brush growing over them, and the broken-down cars and trucks, and the waiting green gums of the woods. I guess I must've been thinking about the remains in the police station – I'd told Bobby I wasn't in the mood for a party – but for a moment I looked at all the decorations and reckoned it was kind of like someone had put make-up on a skeleton.

The parade was called Crooked River's Living History and mostly it was people dressed up and driving down Main Street in the backs of trucks. An Indian family went first, in their native costumes, beating a pow-wow drum and singing. Then came Mr Haney, with two other men, dressed as voyageurs. They were holding paddles, pretending to paddle the truck along, and singing French songs. One of their hats fell off when the truck's wheels went into a pothole. The trappers came next, with buckskins and beaver hats, and then a truck with a canoe on it. Wade Magnussen, who worked at the gas station, was standing beside the canoe holding an axe in one hand and a sign saying 'Pioneer Hotel' in the other. He was meant to be Clarence.

As each truck went past someone in the front threw handfuls of candy out the window onto the sidewalk for the kids to collect. There were hardly enough kids to collect it all and Bobby was having a field day picking it up. He must've filled two bagfuls in the first five minutes. By the time the miners' and loggers' trucks went past he was bugging Sarah and me to get him another bag. It was then that Billy arrived on the back of the floatplane truck, with two other bush pilots who worked for Buddy. They were wearing white scarves and leather hats with goggles resting on top of them like real old-fashioned pilots. The two other pilots were waving and smiling at the people clapping and cheering them, but Billy wasn't. He was staring right at the three of us and his eyes looked so big and round it was like he was actually wearing his goggles.

When the truck came up opposite us he started shouting. At first you couldn't hear him properly because of the clapping and cheering but after a second or two the clapping and cheering had died right down. Bradley Cain, who was driving, must've thought something had happened and stopped the truck.

'It's a disgrace, a fucking disgrace, you flaunting it in front of me like this in public – playing happy frigging families with that retard. That's my kid, you bitch, and I don't give a flying fuck what you say about it. He's mine and I'm allowed to take him whenever I frigging want. There's no law . . .'

And he would've carried on except the crash flung him and one of the other pilots right off the side of the truck.

The last truck was made up to look like a train car. They'd collected some old iron ore pellets and filled the back with them. Buddy was sitting on top of them on a chair holding his key, and there was a little pine tree stuck in them too. Clyde Fraser, who was driving, must've been so busy throwing candy out the window he hadn't noticed the pilots' truck stopped in front of him and ploughed right on into the back of it. It was lucky he was going slow, but it still hit hard enough to send Billy and the other pilot flying. And Buddy had got flung right off the back of the truck and was sitting there in the middle of a pothole in Main, holding his key. He wasn't beaming any more and he sure didn't look like no King of Big Rock Candy Mountain.

When I turned around I found that Sarah and Bobby had gone. They must've gone in a real hurry because Bobby had dropped his bags of candy and they were lying on the sidewalk, half-spilled. I gathered them up for him and was going to start heading back to the Poplars but instead I found my footsteps taking me back towards the river and then back towards number one O'Callaghan Street. It was like I couldn't help it, like they just took me there of their own accord. I went through the gate, into the garden, past the old boards left over from the hotel, in through the porch, and then sat down in the living room beneath the Helsinki picture. The sky hadn't changed in the picture, it never does – it was as blue and perfect and full of light as ever and the stars still shone on the cathedral's dome.

I was thinking of my dad then, even though I always try my best not to. (Sometimes if I try real hard it's like he isn't there – or only a bit there, like a drawing someone's half-rubbed out with an eraser. Sometimes he'd been like that in real life. I remember once how, when his circle of tempers was getting so bad he couldn't come down from his room upstairs, he called me up there. When I went in I found him sitting in a rocking chair, going back and forth with his head cupped in his hands. I could see he was crying because his fingers were wet.

'Eli,' he said. 'I'm so sorry, Eli. I'm so sorry.'

I didn't say nothing. I was scared of him because he was crying.

'I'm so sorry, Eli. I've not been here for you. I know that. I've not been a proper father to you. But I'm trying, I promise you. Jesus Christ I'm trying.'

And I still couldn't say nothing because I was scared and he just kept rocking back and forth.)

The stars were still shining on the dome and the sky was its perfect blue the same as it always was and I was thinking, even though I didn't want to, what it was that he found so dark in a picture so full of light. And suddenly it came to me: it was that it never changed; he hated it *because* it never changed. I thought I could understand it now. He'd seen it for real and it must have looked even more perfect to him than it did in the picture. He'd just got married and was there on his honeymoon. Why don't you go somewhere warm, everyone had said when he and my mum decided to go. But her grandfather was from Finland, the same as my nana, so they went to Helsinki.

I never knew my mum. I guess I must have seen her but I don't remember it. After I came out all weak and blue with the cord wrapped around my neck I got better but she got worse. Maybe it was the fifty below and her not being able to be in the hospital. I don't know why. Nobody ever talked about it. Nobody ever mentioned her. My dad wouldn't let them. I had a mum for a few weeks and then she was gone. It was like she'd never even existed. There wasn't any trunk in the basement which was hers, packed with her special things and looking like she might come back and say, 'I forgot my trunk.' There was nothing. Dad got rid of everything – everything except the Helsinki picture, which wasn't hers in any case.

Virgil told me once that that was just his way of trying not to look back. But I don't reckon it ever worked for him. I could sort of understand that now, looking at the picture. He couldn't stop his circle of tempers and they were always spinning him around this perfect place and time he could see and remember but was never able to go back to. And the perfect place never changed. He could see and remember it but he could never change it – make it not so perfect, the same as real life – until it became like his own Bermuda Triangle and he couldn't get out of it. Not until the day he took Clarence's Luger out of the trunk and shot himself with it.

Nana, Virgil and me were all in the kitchen when we heard the shot. Nana sort of crumpled when she heard it, like *she'd* been shot. Virgil ran upstairs. The chair was still rocking back and forth when he went in and found him.

Don't look back. I think I know that now, Virgil. I think I understand that. If something can't be changed then it's best not to look for it. Sometimes you've got to leave the lost things hidden.

That night I tried to sleep on the porch. I hadn't slept there in a long time, not since I'd gone to live at the Poplars, and part of me kept worrying I should be heading back there. I had Bobby's candy and he'd be wanting it. And then there was Sarah and what Billy had shouted. But I reckoned nothing would be happening with Billy: he wouldn't be giving her any more black eyes tonight; I could hear Buddy and him hollering at each other over the fence at number two O'Callaghan Street.

It was warm on the couch and the screens were still good enough to keep most of the bugs out, but I missed the night trains going through and the sounds of the others being shunted on the tracks.

I missed Virgil and Jim too, sitting out on the porch talking. If I closed my eyes and concentrated real hard, though, it was like I could hear them again and even smell the whiskey in their glasses: Virgil asking about Clarence and Jim answering him. That's the way it usually went. It was Virgil's way of looking for him. He must've started out looking for him for real, with the search parties, and then afterwards on his own in the bush, but by the time I was around this asking questions must've seemed the only way left. It was as if it were a riddle or something; as if he'd found one of his books with a bunch of its pages missing.

So when did he start building it? Virgil asked.

I can't be a hundred per cent on that front, Virgil, Jim said. I reckon a week or two after she left. But I couldn't be sure, nobody could. He didn't tell nobody what he was up to.

But somebody must've noticed. Somebody must've noticed something.

We started guessing something was up pretty soon, but nothing definite, nothing for sure. It was a different place back then, Virgil, you've got to understand that. There was what? maybe a hundred and fifty of us living here – at most. When you went out into the bush that was your business. Nobody was going to ask you why and where. And there wasn't such a big chance you were going to bump into anybody out there neither. I mean, there were shackers who lived nothing more than a couple of miles out of town who I only saw once or twice a year when they came in to Schieder's store to buy supplies. And don't forget, it was before the diversion, before the mine. Eye Lake wasn't no lake then, Virgil, with a road going to it and everything. It was just a part of the bush that the Crooked River ran through before it flowed into Red Rock Lake and then back out again and through town. They hadn't dammed it yet and detoured it into the loop round Red Rock.

So when did people start noticing something was up?
Virgil asked.

I reckon it would have been when he started neglecting the hotel. It wasn't anything big or nothing, not to begin with, not the first few years. It was only little things – like forgetting to fix a leak or two in the roof or a creaking floorboard here and there – things you maybe wouldn't have even noticed somewhere else. But your dad was real proud of that hotel, Virgil. He'd built it with his bare hands, in the middle of nowhere, and he was proud of every board and beam of it. Sometimes you'd hear him saying to the railroad men in the dining room how if he hadn't taken the chance and built it he'd still have been picking tobacco down there in Sarnia. He'd made something of himself here and he was happy with what he'd made. There might've been bears and wolves roaming about outside in the garden but he made sure there wasn't a fork out of place in the kitchen. So we noticed when them little things weren't getting done. He'd always spent time out in the bush – doing a bit of prospecting and trapping and hunting on the side, the same as most men here did – but before he'd always paid his full attention to his hotel.

So you knew something was up but you didn't know exactly what.

That's it. That's the nail on the head. There was a bunch of little things but we didn't know what they were adding up to. Like there was the time me and Jake Ottertale went fishing up the Crooked River. We'd gone a few miles up – further than we normally did: we

134

were looking for new spots, out towards where the eastern shore of Eye Lake is now. We were casting from the banks of the river when Jake says to me that he hears a noise. I listened for a bit, and sure enough I could hear it too: a sawing noise. They aren't cutting this side of the river? I asked Jake, and he said no, they weren't even planning to. So both of us head into the bush, following the noise, and we haven't gone far when we come upon Clarence, sawing away at a big red pine with his old bow saw (there weren't many who had their own chain saws back then, mostly just the lumberjacks), his shirtsleeves rolled up and about a million bugs taking a dip in the sweat dripping down his face and neck.

'Hey there, Clarence,' we said, kind of sheepish. 'How's she going?'

And he turns his head around like he isn't even surprised to see us and says, 'Hi there, boys. You've come a long ways up river today.' He doesn't even stop his sawing.

'Just looking for new fishing spots,' I told him.

'Well,' he says, stopping his sawing for a second and rubbing a few hundred of the bugs off his neck, 'I'll be honest with you boys. I've tried this stretch myself and I've never had much luck at all. One or two at most. Hardly bigger than minnows.' Which, as you well know, is what every fisherman tells you if he's got his own eye on a spot and wants to keep it to himself.

'I hear they're catching a ton down by the narrows on the other side of town,' he says. 'Can barely get their hooks in the water before they get bitten – that's what they been telling me.'

And Jake and me stood there for a moment or two longer until we started to get the feeling Clarence didn't want us around, like we were a couple of those bugs and he was trying to brush us off. He wasn't being unfriendly or nothing like that: he just looked like a man who had a hell of a lot to do.

That was a month or so after the picnic and we didn't think much of it at the time. We didn't even get around to asking what he was doing. He was chopping wood. There was nothing special about a man chopping wood in Crooked River, especially one who had a whole hotel to keep heated. He'd found himself a good stand of tall red pines there by the river. It was only afterwards it occurred to us that usually you wouldn't cut good lumber like that for burning. And besides, in Crooked River terms that was a hell of a long ways to go to get firewood.

And then of course there was his correspondence.

His correspondence, Virgil said. With who? About what?

Well, Jim said, it was easy enough to figure some of that out afterwards, the same as everything else, but at the time we didn't have much of a clue. All we knew was that every Friday afternoon, at five minutes to five on the button, Clarence would walk the twenty feet from the front step of his hotel to Schieder's store and hand Schieder a letter and the money for a stamp. The highway didn't reach us then so all our mail came and went by train five o'clock Friday. There was always quite a bustle around Schieder's at that time, with everyone coming to send or collect their mail. One of the railroad men would bring the sack of incoming mail from the train to Schieder's, and Jake, who used to help out in the store, would take the sack of outgoing mail over to the train. It was a real social occasion, with everyone hovering about the store waiting to see if they'd got something and, if they had, oftentimes reading it then and there and sharing their news with others. The mail was a big deal back then. We didn't have no TV and there was only two radios in town, so whatever news you had of the world came in that sack.

Clarence treated the occasion different from everyone else though. For a start, it was only twenty feet for him to walk but he got real dressed up for the journey. He'd wear his Sunday finest – a black suit, polished shoes, a hat . . . hell, even his buttons were polished. You'd see them glinting like pieces of silver as he walked across the dirt of the road. It was as if whoever he was sending his letter to would know just what he looked like when he sent it. And when he got to the store he wouldn't say anything, only nod politely at the people grouped outside who said hello to him, and he'd look so serious and determined and solemn that when he got near the door they'd sort of open a path through for him, like the parting of the Red Sea. Then he'd hand his letter – always just the one letter – over the counter to Schieder, as if he were trusting him with a nugget of gold.

Schieder must've known where those letters were going – he must've seen the address on them – but being responsible for the post back then was like being a doctor or lawyer, as though you'd taken one of them oaths of secrecy. Where something got sent was strictly *between you and the postmaster. So Schieder never spoke to nobody about Clarence's letters and Clarence never spoke to nobody about them neither. And when he got one back – which he didn't get that regular, not as regular as he sent them – every month or two maybe, often less – he didn't open it there and then like most other folks did, but would put it carefully in the inside pocket of his suit jacket and walk slow and steady back to the hotel, as if he wasn't in much of a hurry to read it at all. Not that that fooled anybody: every week, after he'd handed over his letter, he'd go wait quietly in the corner of the store for the time it took for the train to arrive and Jake to bring back the mail sack and everybody else to get their mail, rubbing his hands together while he waited like he was nervous, until there was just him left.*

'Is there something for me?' he'd ask then. And if Schieder said no he'd pause a second and ask, 'Are you sure?' And Schieder, being polite, would hold open the empty sack for him to look.

I guess it must have been her, Virgil said.

I don't see who else it could've been, Virgil. He didn't have any correspondence before that picnic, not that I knew of. And he sure didn't fancy himself up and walk to Schieder's store every Friday afternoon.

So that piece of paper, the one you saw her put in his hand that day on the platform, it must've been an address.

It must have, Jim agreed.

And he never said what was in those letters.

He never said a word about them. But they must've promised something to him because he kept turning up like clockwork at Schieder's store five-to-five every Friday afternoon and he kept trekking out there into the bush every day too. By the fall a piece of guttering had broke on the hotel and when Jake and me went back up the river to check for fishing spots we found he'd cut down a good part of that red pine stand already. It was plain to us then he was building something.

But you didn't know what.

No, we didn't know what. I guess we figured maybe he was building a new hotel or something. It didn't seem that promising a spot, out there in the middle of nowhere, but hell, he'd sure got it right the first time! I guess we figured he knew something we didn't, like they were going to put in a highway out there or something. Oh, and there was another thing I almost forgot. He didn't play his fiddle again that whole summer. In fact he didn't play it for a good long while after.

How long?

A good few years, I reckon, Jim said.

'And how long was he out there building for?'

'Fifteen years. About the same time he didn't play his fiddle for, now I come to think of it.

Jesus, Virgil said. Fifteen years! He spent fifteen years building it! And the letters? Was he still getting the letters that whole time?

He was still getting some the first few years. They kind of trailed off slowly after that – you know, one every six months and then one every year – so nobody really noticed exactly when they stopped coming altogether. But he still kept on sending his as regular as clockwork. And each time he went in to send them he'd wait just the same as before until everybody else had collected their mail, and then he'd ask Schieder, 'Is there something for me? Are you sure?' And when Schieder died he'd ask his son – who was running the store then – the exact same thing.

And when did you know what it was? Virgil asked.

When what was?

What he was building.

Well, after about ten years it already looked like no building we'd ever seen before. The whole thing was made of logs, red pine logs, and it was three storeys high. There was a high wide door at the front and who knows how many rooms inside – we could just see the windows, and there were plenty of them, cut out of the wood. God knows how he did it, Virgil! God knows how he stuck at it! Those logs were real big and he cut and hauled and hoisted every one of them himself, with just a block and tackle. He built it with his bare hands and his sweat and nothing else – with no architect or plans to work with either, just a picture he had in his head, I reckon. Of course he'd built the hotel himself too, but that was different. He'd seen what he was going to build beforehand with the hotel, you could tell; he must've looked at other places and copied them. And once he'd done the foundations, he'd had boards and nails and cut timber brought down the river for him to work with. He had that hotel up and finished in a year. There's all the difference in the world between putting up a frame and nailing on boards, and hauling twenty-foot logs and notching them and hoisting them into place one by one by one until they're three storeys high, thirty feet high. All the difference in the world! And you could tell that too: there were a bunch of buildings that looked the same as that hotel but there were none that looked anything like this one. And it wasn't even finished yet.

Of course, the tower, said Virgil. There was still the tower?

That's right, Jim said. There was still the tower, or the turret – call it what you will. He started on that after ten years. It was built onto the left of the building – as you went upriver – and every time you went up that way to look it'd be a little higher. Because by now me and Jake and other folks from town weren't even pretending to find new fishing spots: we were going there to look at Clarence's building and how it was getting on. We'd bring back reports when we returned to town. 'How high?' people would ask. Ten feet it was in the first year, then twenty in the second, then thirty in the third – the same height as the building's roof – until at last it was almost forty feet by the fifth year and he stopped after that. It was finished then.

And you knew what it was then?

When that tower thing was done we had a pretty good idea. It was a castle, or what Clarence guessed one would look like. We started calling it Clarence's castle. And for those of us who'd been at the picnic that day it wasn't so hard to put the two and two of it together. As soon as he'd finished the tower he cleared a field in front of his castle, right down to the banks of the river, and started seeding it with grass and flowers. It was clear as day then,

Virgil. It was his version of that castle on the banks of the Danube. It was how he'd imagined it. And he'd built it for her! He'd built it for her and it was a damn sight more real than the one he'd heard about that day fifteen years before. I wish you could've seen it, Virgil. It was really something.

I have seen it. I've seen it in a picture, Virgil told him. He had a picture taken.

I never knew he kept that, said Jim. Well, I'm glad you got something, Virgil. I'd like to see that picture again one day myself, to remind me of it. It really was something. And it was only there that one summer.

Again? said Virgil.

It was me that took it, said Jim.

Snow Creatures

The world didn't end that winter after George said it would. It was a bad winter though, bad enough to make you think what the end of the world might look like if it did come. The snow that fell on Halloween was just the first of a whole pile of it that fell through November and December. Almost every day it was falling, until everywhere was covered in heavy blankets of it. It settled thick on the roofs of the houses and the sidewalks and the ice of the river. It covered the baseball field and the roundhouse and the gravel pit. It covered everywhere and everything. Outside the museum the steam train looked like a snow sculpture and the mining drill was barely a lump in the blanket, like the princess's pea. You couldn't see where our garden was or the planks from the old hotel, only a path dug out to the road through banks that got steeper and steeper every day. On Main Street the hillbilly's smile had gone – there were just a few rows of dirty grey teeth and the white spaces of the empty lots and, beyond, the black-and-white gums of the woods. Every branch on every tree was bowed down under the snow and sometimes the only thing you could hear was clumps of it falling to the ground. It got so high by the end of December it was like the whole town was becoming invisible, like there were no roads, no houses, nothing, and everyone had to shovel furiously to show it was still there. And then after Christmas it stopped and the real cold arrived.

Even for us who were all used to the cold, it was bad. I remember how it hurt my lungs when I breathed and froze the hair on my head and the inside of my nostrils. Virgil never stopped hauling logs down to the basement for the wood stove, and at night the basement sounds got mixed up with sounds of cracking and groaning outside my window as everything froze harder and harder. Nana always used to leave breadcrumbs out in the garden in the winter to feed the birds, but this winter they went quiet and still on the branches of the crab apple tree and didn't fly down to eat the crumbs. After a day or so we realized they'd been frozen solid on the tree. We left them there till spring – their songless beaks half open, their feathers covered in a layer of clear ice like they were sculptures carved out of crystal.

Two loggers, Johnny Lewicki and Ed McKinnon, went through the ice of Eye Lake that winter and drowned. Their bodies were never recovered. Virgil and some other men went out to search for them, and after they found the hole in the ice where they'd gone through – there'd been an air pocket that'd made it weak – Virgil went to pay a visit to the Earl and found him lying frozen to death in his bed. You couldn't tell how long he'd been lying like that, Virgil said. It could have been hours or days or weeks. His blankets were as stiff and frosted white as birch bark.

I thought of him lying there, staring up from his bed the same as Johnny Lewicki and Ed McKinnon were staring up from the bed of Eye Lake, with his little round glasses covered in snowflakes and egg like I remembered them being, until he became a watcher just the same as Johnny and Ed had become.

The beginning of the second week of January was my birthday, two days after Billy's. Billy had a big party for his. Most of the kids from school came, except George. Brenda made a huge cake and Buddy had bought a pile of presents from Thunder Bay. There was a bike and a model plane with batteries that meant it actually flew and a baseball glove and a bunch of other stuff. We couldn't go outside to play because of the cold and Billy had a tantrum because the other kids kept trying to use his new presents, so we all had to go home early.

I didn't have a party for mine. I never usually did and that suited me just fine. I didn't much like being reminded of the forty below and the cord being wrapped around my neck and all that. And besides this was always the worst time of year for my dad and his circle of tempers and so we never made a fuss about me being born.

This year it was especially bad because it was forty below most days and on my birthday it was almost fifty below with the wind. Dad didn't get out of bed at all. Virgil told me he wasn't feeling well and gave me a new fishing reel he said Dad had got me before, when he wasn't feeling as bad. Nana had made me a cake with candles on it and then Virgil said he had a surprise for me.

'You've got a visitor,' he said as I was getting ready to

blow out the candles. And when he opened the porch door George was standing there, wrapped up in about a hundred scarves and hats as if he were a present or something. I couldn't see what was so special about George coming to visit, but he'd hardly been allowed out for months and I hadn't seen him since Halloween, so I guess it was sort of special.

After we'd eaten the cake Virgil and Nana went into the living room and I showed George my new reel. Without his hats and scarves on he looked the same colour as everything outside did, as if he were a snow creature and was meant to be that colour for camouflage. And for a moment I thought maybe this was the weather he was meant for and he only looked different and strange when the snow wasn't there, like the rabbits who got their winter coats too early in the year so you could see them standing out in the bush with their fur white against the grey and brown and pale green colours of the fall, thinking they were invisible when they weren't. I asked him where he'd been and why he hadn't been out.

'I *have* been out,' he said, puffing up his skinny chest. 'I've been out *lots* of times.'

I told him I hadn't seen him.

'That's because they're secret,' he said.

'What's secret?'

'The *expeditions*,' he said.

He told me him and his dad went out twice a week sometimes. They walked along the frozen river to where the underground place was, carrying cans and stuff in their pockets.

'It's important we don't look too conspicuous. That it's not too obvious,' he said. 'We use snowshoes and everything, like real polar explorers,' he added proudly.

I didn't think there was anything special about wearing snowshoes but I didn't say nothing because he looked so pleased with himself.

'Dad says it's important that everything's prepared,' he said.

I didn't bother asking for what because I knew he'd start talking about the end of the world again and I didn't want him to talk about that. I didn't want him to say how maybe I could go to the underground place with them, and then for me to think about Nana and Virgil and Dad left behind in the end of the world and then to feel mad about that and mad with George, like I had before. I just wanted him to come to the door with his new exhibits and for us to go to the railroad bridge and fish with bobbers and all that old stuff. I must've been quiet for a while thinking that because then he asked me, all worried, 'You haven't told anyone, have you?'

'No,' I said.

'You have to promise, Eli. You have to swear on your . . . You have to swear on something really important!'

'I won't tell nobody,' I said. I just wanted everything to be like it was before.

'Dad made me take an oath,' he said, 'which is a really important promise. I can't even tell my mum.'

'I promise I won't tell nobody.'

It was OK then and George got onto talking about other stuff. He said he'd read in a special edition of one of his *National Geographic*s about these explorers who'd travelled north of us, up into the Hudson Bay and beyond, near the North Pole, looking for a way to sail around the world and things like that. He was really excited about it. He told me about how there was nobody but Eskimos up there and polar bears and huge fields of ice that went on and on for miles and miles. He told me about giant icebergs and days that lasted through the whole night, when the sun never set and the light never went away. He told me about how some of the explorers had never come back and how they'd found empty ships frozen in the ice and old bones hidden beneath the snow. He was excited in the same way he got excited when Mrs Arnold told us about Clarence stepping out of his canoe that first time – like he was imagining himself there in a place that was fresh and new and full of exhibits.

When I looked outside through the window at where it was fifty below I reckoned we were already plenty north enough. But I didn't say nothing about it and was glad I didn't, because when he left and I watched him walk down the path dug out of the drifts in our garden, beneath the crab apple tree where the frozen birds still stood on the branches, he looked right there somehow, like I'd thought before, like he fitted into this world of ice and snow. And I could picture him there in the north, beneath the sun that never set, in the light that never changed, walking through the white fields, past the icebergs, like it was his home.

After the end of January George had two homes. Gracie moved out of their place to a house near the museum. She didn't want to live with Mr McKenzie any more.

'I've had enough,' I heard her telling Virgil one day in our kitchen, while Nana was making porridge on the stove. 'I can't go on like this.'

So during the week George didn't live over the road, he lived with Gracie, and I never got to see him. On the weekends he came back to stay with his dad – except I hardly ever saw him then neither, because George was still kept inside, behind the tall fence, or else they were out on their expeditions, I guessed. It was OK though. When I did see him, George said he was finishing with his home schooling in the spring and coming back to normal school. His allergies were better, he said. And I was a bit sad then because I remembered we wouldn't be in the same class any more on account of the cord being wrapped around my neck.

Nana's Quilt

I must've slept some because when I opened my eyes there was daylight falling through the screens of the porch windows onto my quilt. It was a quilt Nana had made by sewing together different pieces of cloth. They were square-shaped mostly, and each piece had different patterns and colours and pictures – some were red with white polka dots and others had trees and animals on them and others had little houses like the ones that were made of candy from fairy-tale books. They reminded me that I still had Bobby's bags of candy.

The quilt was like a jigsaw. When I was a kid I used to look at it as I lay in bed and try fitting the pieces together in my head. I tried doing that this morning but I couldn't concentrate because of the banging noises coming from next door.

Billy was standing in the back yard of number two O'Callaghan Street hitting the back of his truck with a spanner. There didn't seem to be nothing wrong with it but he was hitting it and saying, 'fucking useless old piece of shit', even though it was almost brand new. Billy lived in a place Buddy had built right behind his place and called 'the annexe'. It was just another house really, not as big as number two but still a house. Buddy had built it for Billy to live in when he was just twenty. 'Keeping the Three Bs a unit,' he'd said when he was building it.

Buddy was standing in the back door of number two and he must've said something because Billy stopped banging the truck for a second and turned around and shouted, 'I don't give a shit about that. Just tell her. She can whistle Dixie for all I care. She can live in the street! And don't tell *me* what's right or wrong. I know what's frigging right and wrong and what she's doing sure as hell isn't right. This fucking truck . . .'

'This fucking . . .' said Billy, and I ducked my head down below the fence before him or Buddy saw me. As I was heading out the garden I spotted Brenda staring out the upstairs window. She wasn't smiling.

On Main there was nobody about. There were bits of leftover cake and hotdogs and corncobs from the birthday party lying around on the sidewalk. A warm breeze was blowing from the west, covering them in a thin red dust. When I reached the tracks I looked at the prairie flowers that'd come from the west as well, and thought about Sarah's hand. It seemed like I could still feel it against my own hand, as if her skin had left a kind of dust behind too – soft and invisible.

Back at the Poplars Bobby was fishing for minnows off the dock.

'Any luck?' I asked.

'I got two,' he said, pointing to the bucket beside him without lifting his head up from where he was staring into the water at his line. 'Shiners.' At the bottom of the bucket I saw a quick flash of silver.

'I brought you your candy,' I said, pulling the bags out of my pockets. He didn't seem that interested in it. He was more interested in the minnows.

'We had to leave in a hurry because of my dad,' he said, still not taking his eyes off his line.

'I know.'

'My mum's worried about him.'

'I know.'

'She thinks he wants to take me away to live with him at Grampa's place.'

I couldn't think what to say for a while after that.

'How'd you like to go proper fishing?' I asked.

When we went to look for Sarah to ask if Bobby could go we found her in the office on the telephone. She was listening real carefully to what was being said. Her eyes looked as black and mad as the eyes of the mother of the baby owl I'd found on my way into town. When we asked her if it was OK she nodded quickly and waved us away.

There was an old wooden rowboat behind the Hematite Conference Room that I used for fishing sometimes, when I was going to spots that weren't too far.

I dragged the boat down to the beach and let Bobby carry one of the oars. There was still a bit of a breeze blowing but it only ruffled the water and made it dance and shine in the sunlight. We set off, keeping close to the eastern shore and weaving our way between the bare slippery trunks of the trees that stuck up out of the surface. Sometimes the oars brushed against their branches under the water. After a while Bobby said he wanted to try rowing so I showed him how and let him have a go. At first we just went from side to side, and then in circles, but he got the hang of it real quick and soon we were going slowly forwards again. Now and again I couldn't help looking down over the side of the boat, through the dancing, shining surface, to where you could see branches swaying under the water over the dark edges of drop-offs.

Pretty soon we'd gone around the first point and I told Bobby to take us in closer to the shore, into the little bay behind it. We swapped places and I put a spinner – a Ruby Eye – on the rod I'd given him and trolled us back and forth a few times, around a reef I knew was there; but we didn't have any luck so I rowed us further on towards the point at the other side of the bay, almost opposite the second island. At the side of the point I stopped the boat and tied it to a tree trunk sticking out of the water and got some jigs out of my tackle box. I put a white-and-red one on for Bobby, and I used Virgil's home-made one that looked like a south sea idol. 'You let it go right down to the bottom,' I told him. 'Then reel in the slack and keep jerking it up a bit and letting it fall back down so it touches the bottom.'

'How will I know if I got one?'

'You'll feel a little tug.'

'What do I do then?'

'You set it.'

'What's setting?'

'It's when you give it a real hard jerk – to get the hook stuck in the fish's mouth. The same as with the minnows.'

'But I can't see my bait.'

'You don't need to see it. You'll know when to set it when you feel the tug.'

Bobby was so excited he kept setting his line every time he felt his jig touch the bottom.

'But I felt something,' he said every time.

'That's just the bottom,' I kept telling him.

'But how'll I know when it's a fish?'

'You'll know.'

The breeze died down as we jigged and soon the water was totally calm and flat. There was an eagle perched on a tree by the point, waiting for fish guts. It was so still it was like everything was waiting: the trees and the water and sky – everything. This is one of my favourite things about fishing, this waiting: the hush and the stillness of it, like everything has come to a stop and is holding its breath.

Bobby wasn't quite as happy with the waiting. 'When will I know if I got one?' he kept asking.

'You'll know,' I kept telling him.

After a while it seemed like the only things moving were the tips of our rods as we jigged and a thin strip of water to our left, that rippled slightly even though there was no breeze at all. Bobby asked me why it was moving when the rest of the water was calm.

'It's the river,' I told him.

'What river?'

'The Crooked River.'

I explained to him how it flowed under the lake from the inlet where it came in, just around the point, and that even though it was mixing with the lake's water it still kept a kind of course, and when it was calm like this you could sometimes see its current.

'Where does it go?' he asked.

I told him it went over to Jackfish Bay, to the outlet, and then looped around on the detour until it joined its old course again through town. But it used to go a different way, I said. It used to go through where the dam was now and then through Red Rock Lake – when it was still a lake and Eye Lake wasn't nothing but the river running through the woods.

'They told us about that in school,' he said. 'But they never said you could still see it.'

'Water's a bit like a dog . . .' I told him.

'What's that?' he asked, pointing. We'd drifted a few feet around the point and the tower of Clarence's castle was sticking right out of the water.

'That's the castle my grandfather built,' I told him. It felt good to be able to tell someone.

'Why's it . . .' he started asking. And then he set his line and it stayed set.

'You got one,' I said. 'You better start reeling.'

He reeled so fast he almost skinned his knuckles against the spool of his reel.

*

The whole way back Bobby couldn't stop looking at his fish. He kept reaching down into the bottom of the boat to touch it, as if he was making sure it was still there and it was still a real fish. It was a good-sized walleye and the golden scales along its sides shone and glittered in the sunlight.

'Why are its eyes like that?' he asked me, prodding one of them with his finger. They were black around the edges with a big, kind of milky, circle filling most of the eye, reflecting back the light and colours like a huge pearl.

'So it can see better in the dark,' I told him. 'Mostly they're evening biters. You're lucky to get one so early.'

'And that's why they call them walleyes?'

'It sure is. Some people call them Pickerel too.' As if recognizing its name, the fish began flopping around on the bottom of the boat.

'I don't want to go there,' Bobby suddenly said.

'Where?'

'To town. To live with Dad at Grampa Buddy's place.'

'Well, maybe you won't have to.'

'I don't want to, Eli. Dad never wanted me there before, not ever. I won't go there. I won't.'

'I'm pretty sure you won't have to. Your dad's a strange one like that. He mostly wants things when he thinks he can't have them or someone else has them. It's just his way. He'll forget about the whole thing soon enough.'

'I heard Mum say he wasn't my dad.'

'That's not my business, Bobby.'

'You won't let him take me?'

'It's not my business, Bobby. I can't do nothing. It's not my business.'

And then Bobby was staring down at his fish again and I could see the tears falling onto its golden scales.

When we got back Sarah was waiting for us at the landing.

'Where the hell have you been?' she asked when Bobby and me got out of the boat.

Bobby said nothing. He hadn't said nothing for a while. He was cradling that walleye in his arms like it was a teddy bear.

'We went fishing,' I said.

'You went fishing,' she repeated. Her eyes were like the mother owl's again. '*You went fishing!* You take my son out for the whole frigging afternoon and don't bother to tell me. Do you know what I've been thinking? *Do you know?* I've been frantic. I've been running about the site looking for him like a headless fucking chicken. Do you know, Eli? *Do you know?*'

I said I'd tried telling her when she was on the phone but she was so mad it was like she couldn't hear me.

'Come on, Bobby,' she said, grabbing him by the arm. 'We're going.'

Bobby kept hold of his fish and traipsed beside her. She was walking so fast he could hardly keep up and she kept stopping and pulling him along.

The colour and brightness had gone out of the fish's scales; I was going to show him how to clean it, I thought.

Then I pulled the boat up on the shore and when I went to tie it to a tree I realized I was so miserable I could hardly concentrate enough to tie the knot.

That evening I went to check on Clarence's castle. Before I'd even reached the shore I could see through the spruce and pine branches that it was even further out of the water. The tower was plain in view, and most of the third-floor too. The logs were a greeny-brown colour from the slime and a family of ducks were swimming in and out of the third-floor windows like they were the doors of their house.

When I reached the shore I could see even more proof of just how far the water had dropped. The roots of trees were hanging out in the air and the tops of dead-heads were poking out through the mud. I sat on a rock, waiting for the moment when the sun would drop down onto the horizon of the far shore and silhouette the second island and turn everything golden like the scales of Bobby's walleye when it first came out of the water. I hoped everything would feel better in those soft moments of light.

I didn't even hear Sarah coming through the woods from the trail. The first thing I heard was her saying, 'So this must be your special spot then, Eli.'

She was standing right behind me.

'I guess so,' I said.

'Do you come here often?'

'I never used to,' I said.

'I saw you walking down the trail in this direction,' she said. 'I was hoping I'd find you.'

She sat beside me on the rock.

'Look, I'm really sorry about flying off the handle before, Eli. I didn't mean to, I promise. Bobby explained how you asked when I was on the phone but I must have been so preoccupied I didn't register what you were saying. Things are all kind of going to shit at the moment and I'm a bit on edge.' She gave a funny-sounding laugh then and said, 'More than kind of and more than a bit.'

'What things?'

'Well, for starters that was Buddy on the phone. He wants me and Bobby out of the Poplars. He sounded embarrassed and was pretty apologetic about it – and I know it's just Billy being a vindictive prick – but the fact of the matter is we're going to have to move out. And I don't really know what the hell we're going to do. There's my parents' place in Calgary, but I don't want to take Bobby out of school here – he's settled and he likes it.'

'He doesn't want to go,' I said.

'No, he doesn't. Plus Billy's got some nutty idea into his head about claiming custody. He thinks Bobby can go live with him and Buddy and Brenda in town. I swear to God, Eli, first he wants us out here and then he wants Bobby back in town and me out of the picture. It's insane. It's fucking insanity.'

'Why did you tell him?' I asked.

'Tell him what?'

'About Bobby not being his kid.' She was quiet for a long time then. She was wearing sandals and started making a little hole in the dirt with her toe.

'Look, I don't expect you to understand this, Eli. I don't

expect *anyone* to understand this. But once upon a time I wanted Billy to be his father. I know it sounds stupid but I wanted Billy to be his father more than anything. And he was. To all purposes Billy *was* his dad. And then he lost all interest in being a dad, in being anything to either of us, so it just sort of clicked – why not tell him the truth, what the hell of the difference would it make? And how fucking typical of Billy. He decides he wants to be Bobby's dad the moment he finds out he isn't.'

The sun was moving closer to the horizon of the far shore, turning it into a shadowy outline that sloped gently up and down with the tops of a few tall poplars sticking up out of it like cowlicks.

'I'm sorry you've got messed up in all this shit, Eli.'

'That's OK,' I said. 'I reckon I understand.'

'You know, you shouldn't listen to Billy and all them. You're not stupid, Eli. I'd say you're a whole bunch smarter than a lot of them.'

Then she took hold of my hand again and turned to look over towards the far shore the same as me.

'What *is* that?' she asked, pointing over at the tower.

'That's my grandfather Clarence's castle,' I said. It felt really good to tell someone at last, just the same as it had when I told Bobby, and I was really glad it was her I was telling it to.

'A *castle?*' she said, looking back at me.

'That's what the old-timers used to call it, Clarence's castle. It's what he meant it to be. He built it all by himself.'

'How much more of it is under there?'

'That's just the tower part,' I said. 'The big part is still under there . . . like an iceberg.'

'Jesus,' she said. 'Why did he build it?'

'It's a long story,' I said.

'A *castle*,' she said, slowly shaking her head. 'Jesus . . . this place!'

The sun had come down low onto the horizon now and the green of the trees behind us was beginning to turn golden. It was so still and hushed we didn't say anything for a while. After a bit, though, I wanted to tell Sarah more about the castle.

'I didn't know it was here until a few days back,' I said. 'I knew it was somewhere but I didn't know exactly where. And then the water started dropping. I don't know why it's dropping so fast.'

'You've not heard?' she said.

'Heard what?'

'Buddy told me on the phone – I guess he was trying to sweeten the pill a bit. There's a breach in the dam. A hole. A big one. And they're not going to bother fixing it. They're just going to let the water follow its old course. Buddy said the whole of Eye Lake is going to turn into one big swamp in a while, after it drains. I guess he thought that'd kind of put me off staying on at the Poplars anyway.'

'I didn't hear that,' I said.

'Why was it under the water in the first place?' she asked.

'Why was what under the water?'

'Your grandfather's castle, Eli.'

Going Under

That was a long story too. We'd heard most of it in school as kids, in our Crooked River history – about how Buddy Bryce discovered the ore lodes under Red Rock Lake and how they drained it and detoured the river. You could read about it in the museum and look at the pictures: Buddy out on the ice drilling for samples; the rock cuts going through the bush; Buddy and the engineers and everyone else from town waiting for them to blow the final charge to open the diversion; the explosions; the dredgers on the bottom of Red Rock Lake; Buddy coming into town sitting on the first train car of ore, with the little red pine sticking out of it. *A True Northern Entrepreneur*, it said under that picture. You could find out just about all of it almost.

But there was one bit which wasn't in the museum and was never in our school history lessons neither. That was the bit Jim told Virgil – about how he took a picture of the castle, especially for Clarence.

Jim told Virgil it happened in June. The first week in June. He said Clarence had come up to him one night as he was having a drink in the hotel and asked if he'd ever used a camera before.

'No,' Jim said.

'Well, how'd you like to try?' Clarence said.

The next morning they went up the river to the castle. Clarence didn't say much of anything the whole trip. When they got there he just stood in front of the castle and asked Jim if he could fit him and it into the lens. Jim said he had to go right back to the edge of the river's bank to get them both in.

He clicked the button once and Clarence said, 'That'll do, that'll have to do.'

The funny thing was, Jim told Virgil, he didn't look all that pleased to have finished it, and he didn't act it neither. I mean you'd think after fifteen years working on it he'd be over a second moon! But no. He looked and acted like a man who'd woken up one morning to find one of his legs missing and his dog dead and his wife gone and his house blown down. And the other funny thing was that it wasn't even till the next week that they announced the plans for the diversion and all the trucks and diggers and workers arrived.

It all happened quickly after that, Jim told Virgil. Through the rest of June and July and August it was like a war zone – with the trucks and diggers churning their way into the bush and the blasting of the rock cuts as they prepared the new course for the river. You could hear the dynamite explosions in town. Once, twice, sometimes three times a day. Like a war zone. And of course they were working so fast because the real war was coming – it was already well started – and they needed that iron in a hurry.

As for Clarence, he carried on as if nothing was happening. Every morning, first thing, he'd walk out the front door of his hotel – a door that creaked on its hinges now and shed flakes of blistered paint every time it slammed shut – and down to his rowboat on the bank of the river. He'd taken to wearing his Sunday suit – the one he wore to the post office – every day by then, and it was starting to get frayed around the cuffs and collars. And dusty too, Jim said, real dusty, like everything else in town was getting as the trucks and diggers and men rumbled through it onto the new road into the bush. And there'd be Clarence, paddling past them up the river in his boat, dressed in his suit like he was off to a picnic with the Queen. Every day it was the same. Like clockwork. And at sunset, just as the men and trucks were returning from the bush, you'd see him paddling back.

That went on for the whole summer, Jim said. Through June and July and August. And by then the hotel was in a really bad way. There were more leaks in it than a sieve and tears in the window screens and the paint hanging on for dear life. You'd see the people who still stayed there – and there weren't many by then – come out in the mornings itching themselves and cursing. It was falling apart around him, and it was like your father couldn't even see it any more, Virgil, like it was invisible to him. And the worst part was there was more business in Crooked River that summer than there'd ever been, what with all the men who'd come to work on the diversion. It was like a little gold rush. People were renting their places out and sleeping

164

in tents in their gardens. Schieder's son turned his house into a new hotel. It was a bonanza. And Clarence carried on through it as if none of it was happening, paddling up the river in the morning and back in the evening, with his suit slowly fraying and wearing and filling full of holes.

I guess everyone was so busy making money off the diversion they didn't ask themselves too many questions about what he was up to out there. The castle was finished. There was nothing left to build. But I went out there a few times, pretending to fish but just curious really, wanting to see what on earth he could be doing. And the truth is, Virgil, he was doing nothing, nothing at all – at least none of the times I went to see. He'd be standing there in the doorway of his castle, watching the river. It was like he was waiting.

By August they'd started work on the dam. Clarence couldn't use his boat to reach the castle then; he had to trek out there through the bush. His suit took a real beating from those treks. After a week or two it was barely a set of rags and he began looking as if he were a hobo who'd just jumped off one of the trains. But still he carried on, like clockwork – heading out at first light, coming back at sunset. By the second week of September they'd finished the dam and the water started rising.

At first you would have thought it was only a spring flood. The river swelled and burst its banks and shallow puddles spread out onto the ground surrounding it. It looked no more than what the melt water might do after a hard winter. I went out there a lot then, to see what was going to happen. Quite a few from town did. We were curious. We'd never seen something like this happen before.

After a few days it wasn't like any spring flood no more. All the lowest, swampiest ground was gone under – all you could see was the brown tops of the cattails bobbing about above it like fishing floats; the spruce and tamaracks were under up to their first branches, as if they'd grown without trunks. Then it started creeping up and up onto the higher ground around the swamps. Boulders and outcrops of rock disappeared. Poplar and birch saplings vanished. The pines began to shrink until they started looking like a bunch of Christmas trees planted in water. It happened quick, quicker than you'd think. You'd walk out there one day and then the next you'd get kind of lost because the ground where you'd stood before was gone. It was like someone had taken a big eraser and started rubbing the whole place out and then drawing in a new one. Stands of the tallest poplars and white pines were suddenly poking out of widening bays and growing fingers, ridges had become reefs and points and headlands, hills were islands, the swamps were already the rippling surface of a lake.

From the doorway of his castle, Clarence watched. I passed by there most days during the flooding, and I'd always stop for a few minutes to look. He must have known I was there, but he never acknowledged me and he didn't much look like he wanted company – or not mine or anyone from town, at least. He watched the river as it came up over its banks and then began creeping up his new lawn, inch by inch, foot by foot, covering the green of the grass and the colours of the flowers he'd planted, until it was right at his feet almost, flowing through the door. And then, finally, he stopped going there.

He never saw it. He never saw his castle go under. I went down there every day myself, because it was really something, that castle, Virgil, it was, and I figured I'd not be seeing it again. The water went through the door and rose up to the first set of windows, then the second, then the third, until it was only the top of the tower left. It had one window, that tower, and I watched it go through it. The next day when I came back to look the whole thing was gone. The water lapped the shore where I was standing and you could see the ripple of the current where the river used to be and the second island and the far, new shore on the other side. But that was all. It was like it'd never been there.

The day after, late in the morning, they blew the rock face on the opposite shore and let the river flow into the new course they'd dug for it. Everybody in town went out to watch that last explosion. It was a real occasion. They lined up on a hill looking down on the rock face, and Buddy, surrounded by the engineers and the workers, got ready to push the trigger to ignite the final charge. There was one big boom and for a few moments the air was full of dust. And then you could hear it, and then you could see it too: the water gushing through the jagged gap in the rock into its new course. It went quick and wild at first, surging into the empty channel, pushing chunks of shattered rock and tree trunks in front of it, before gradually it slowed and quietened down and settled into its new path. After nothing more than a few minutes it was trickling along as peaceful as you like. The floodwaters held steady at the level they'd already reached and the lake, the new lake, glistened and twinkled in the fall sun. If you couldn't have seen the tops of the trees sticking out of the surface and smelled the dynamite fumes hanging in the air, it would've seemed like they'd always been there – just another lake and river, hidden out there in the bush.

Everybody from town came to see it, except for Clarence. He hadn't come out of his hotel since the day the water reached the door of his castle; he'd not even come out on post day, which was the first time he'd missed it in fifteen years. He didn't come out until the afternoon.

Buddy had arranged a big celebration party in his garden for after the explosion. All the engineers were there, and the workmen, and a bunch of people from town. The liquor was flowing freely and everyone was in just about the highest spirits you could imagine. There was a smile on every face. It was pretty much the biggest day in the whole history of Crooked River.

And then a few hours into the party Clarence appeared next door on the steps of the hotel and there was no smile on his face; it was looking about as hard and jagged as the rock cuts the river had just flowed into. His suit was gone and he was wearing normal clothes, a red check shirt and a pair of jeans. Every step creaked as he walked down them. As soon as they saw him most people's voices dropped a notch or two, till it was almost quiet in the

*garden. Buddy walked over to the fence, swaying a little
with the liquor.*

*'Clarence,' he said. 'Good to see you. Please, come on
over. I'll get you a drink. Anything you want. We got
plenty.'*

*Your dad's face never shifted an inch, Virgil. It was
like he didn't even see Buddy, like he didn't see anybody.
It seemed an age before he spoke and when he did his lips
barely moved.*

*'That's most considerate of you,' he said. 'Thank you
for the invitation. But I regret I'll have to pass on it.' His
voice was as cold and bleak as January; you could tell
each one of those words was costing him dear. He had the
same look as when he'd made that noise like the mother
bear and I kind of half expected him to make it again.*

*'We've got plenty,' Buddy said, not so cheery and sure
of himself this time.*

'I'm afraid I have some business to attend to.'

*With that he strode on out onto the sidewalk and past
everybody in Buddy's garden and headed over to the train
stop. The party came back to life then. After a few minutes
it was like everyone had forgotten the whole thing.*

*And I guess in the excitement of the diversion, and
everything that was promised to come after it – all the ore
and the money and the mine – they had half-forgotten.
I don't think they even stopped that day to think how his
castle had gone under. Their minds were on bigger things.
I was the only one who'd seen it disappear.*

*

And so the party went on, all through that afternoon and a long ways into the night. And I don't reckon anyone but me even noticed the five o'clock train to Thunder Bay slowing down as it went through and Clarence climbing up into the caboose. He was gone for two days. That was how long it took him to attend to his business – and it was quite a piece of business too.

What was it? Virgil asked.

It was an advert, Virgil. For a wife. It wasn't so uncommon in those days. There weren't too many spare women in these parts. And there were lots of Finns just come to Thunder Bay then who must've been looking for wives from their old country. I guess Clarence must've sent his advert out with theirs. He was fifty-five years old, Virgil. He'd waited a long time.

The very next summer your mother was getting off the train in Crooked River.

And so, in the end, all Clarence had left of his castle was the picture Jim took; the one sitting in the trunk in the basement. If you look at it closely then you can tell it was taken early in the summer. Even though it's black and white there are signs. To the left of Clarence and the castle is a tall poplar, with its flickering leaves fresh out; later on in the summer they droop and wither some. And below his feet there's the grass he'd seeded, just coming through. And if you look real close then you can see the river too, glinting in the black and white as it curves around from the right through the trees, before it disappears off the edge of the picture.

Fallout

On the morning of the fourth day after George went missing Virgil led me into the living room, away from the men in the kitchen, and said:

'I'm going to be straight with you, Eli. Things aren't looking too good. We haven't found George and time's against us now. I'm going to ask you again – and think as hard as you can – is there anything George said to you, about plans he had or things that were happening – anything at all? It might not seem like it was important but you never know. It might give us a clue. I'm not going to lie to you. This is a bad situation, Eli. This is a really bad situation.'

I looked down at the floor and said nothing. My head felt like there was an iron band tightening around it and my stomach felt like it was going to fall out of me onto the floor. I knew all about bad situations.

'I know he's your friend and you're upset but you have to think, Eli. Anything. Anything at all.'

I kept staring at the floor. My tongue felt like it was too big for my mouth. I wanted to tell him everything. But I couldn't. George had made me promise.

'That's OK,' he said, ruffling the hair on my head. 'I know you've tried. And we're going to keep trying too. We're going to do everything we can.'

The week before George and me had been fishing with bobbers by the railroad bridge. I'd caught a slube and was trying to get my hook out of its mouth without cutting my fingers on its teeth. George wasn't even looking at his bobber. He was telling me about how Eskimos ate raw whale blubber and liked the livers most. He picked a stick up from the bank and threw it into the river like a spear. George McKenzie had mastered the art of polar hunting, he said. It was vital for the success of his expedition that he learned how to survive on the land.

'You're going to scare the fish,' I said.

Eli O'Callaghan was slow to learn the necessities of polar survival. I explained to him the art of harpooning.

He threw another stick into the river. He was wearing the fur hat he'd worn all winter, with big flaps that hung down over his ears. The snow and ice had melted a while back, so it was too warm for it now and I could see beads of sweat dripping down the back of his neck.

'You're not going to catch nothing if you keep throwing those sticks.'

It was vital for his men to learn how to adapt to this wilderness . . .

'You'll have to wear a normal hat when you come back to school,' I told him.

'I'm not coming back,' he said. 'My dad doesn't want

172

me to. He says it's not safe for me in Crooked River any more.'

'Your mum told my nana your allergies were gone.'

'It's not my allergies,' he said. 'It's the *situation*, Eli. It's bad. It's not safe. It's *imminent*. Nobody understands the situation properly, not even my mum.'

'You mean the end of the world.'

The conflict is inevitable. The question isn't if, it's when. Those who don't understand that are living in a fool's paradise, and for those who aren't prepared . . .

'If you're not coming back to school then where are you going to be?'

'I'm going to stay in the underground place, the shelter. I'm going to survive in the bush. I know all about it – Dad and me have been practising the necessary skills.'

George made it sound just like he was going off on another of his trips.

'You have to promise not to tell anybody, Eli.'

'I already promised.'

'Maybe it'd be OK for you to come and visit. I'll ask Dad.'

And then I felt mad again, like before, thinking about the end of the world and Nana and Dad and Virgil.

'I don't want to come,' I said. 'I think it's dumb. I don't reckon there's going to be any end of the world.'

'I don't expect *you* to understand all these things,' George said.

'I reckon I understand just fine. I reckon your dad's nuts, like Billy said.'

George had picked up another stick to throw in the

river, but instead of throwing it he hit me in the face with it. My cheek was stinging. Before I even knew what I was doing I had the slube by the tail, raised it high, and whacked him on the side of the head with it. His hat flew off onto the ground. There was a patch of slime sticking to his hair and oozing down the side of his face.

'I don't want you there anyway,' he shouted, with the slime beginning to drip over his top lip. 'I don't want you to visit – ever. And then you'll all be sorry. Just like dad says. *The whole lot of you'll be sorry. This whole stupid town!*'

After Virgil went back into the kitchen to talk to the rest of the men I sat there thinking for a long time. They weren't ever going to find him. I'd seen their maps and they were looking in the wrong places. Then I started thinking how Mr McKenzie was right there across the street, behind his fence. He knew where George was. He'd taken him there. So why wasn't he there with him? If he reckoned it was the end of the world why wasn't he there in his underground place too?

On the day George went missing they'd gone straight over to see him, Virgil and the search party and Sergeant Hughie. They'd asked him a bunch of questions. Then they'd offered to let him join the search party. When Virgil came back he told Nana that Mr McKenzie had had some kind of nervous breakdown and wasn't much help. He told Dad that Mr McKenzie was a useless fucking lunatic and wasn't fit to be a father.

On the evening of the second day, while I was lying in the porch and the men were in the kitchen looking over their maps and making plans for the next day, I'd seen Mr McKenzie slip out from behind his fence and sneak down to the river. But he must've come back by the following morning because I saw Sergeant Hughie going over there to talk to him some more. Later that same morning Gracie had come by to see Nana. She sat on the couch in the porch and her chest started heaving like she couldn't breathe.

'Oh God,' she kept saying, gulping for breath.

When I walked through the porch and she saw me the gulping got worse.

'Oh God,' she said. 'Oh God.'

And I'd wanted to run over and tell her – that George was OK, that he was living out at the underground place. My head was hurting with wanting to tell her. But I'd promised George.

I sat there thinking for a long time and then decided I was going to go get George myself.

When I got to the river I couldn't find Mr McKenzie's canoe anywhere. I trudged up and down the banks, pushing through the bulrushes, until my shoes were soaked. He must've moved it and hidden it somewhere different. Back at number one O'Callaghan Street the men from the search parties were coming and going all the time, so there was no way I could get Clarence's canoe without them seeing me. Then I remembered how Buddy kept a rowboat on the landing near the railroad bridge that him and Brenda used to go on picnics sometimes.

At first I thought I wouldn't be able to shift it. It was made of heavy, varnished pine, with *3BBB* painted in gold on the side. I heaved and heaved, until eventually I managed to turn it over. There were two frogs sitting underneath and, beside them, two oars.

I don't know how long it took me to drag it to the water. It felt like it took forever. Every few minutes I had to stop and get my breath and when I looked I'd still only be a couple of inches further on than the last time I checked. The line in the sand where I'd dragged it was like the beginning of a word I couldn't spell – I didn't know how I was going to get the pencil to the end of it. And it seemed like the sun was getting higher and higher and at any moment someone was going to walk past and see me.

The moment I got the bow into the water I heard a voice behind me:

'Why are you stealing our boat, Eli?'

I turned around and found Billy sitting there, grinning, near the side of the old bridge. He must've been watching me for a while.

'I'm not stealing it,' I said.

'It sure looks to me like you're stealing it.'

'I'm just borrowing it,' I said. 'I'm going to bring it back.'

'Why are you stealing it?'

'I'm not stealing it.' It was getting later. It was getting close to lunch and since George went missing Nana said

I had to be back for lunch at the right time. When I didn't she came out to look for me.

'I need it for fishing,' I said. 'I've got a new spot.'

'Where's your rod, then?' Billy said. 'Can't go fishing without a rod. I'm going to tell my dad you're stealing our boat.' He looked real pleased with himself when he said that.

'Please,' I said. 'Don't tell him. I'm not stealing it. I'll bring it right back. I promise.'

'That's our boat,' he said, walking down to the bank and grabbing hold of the oarlock. 'And you're stealing it and I'm telling.'

I could hear the sound of one of Buddy's planes taking off in the distance. I didn't know what to do then – I felt like if I didn't go get George right that second I'd never get the chance again – so I picked up one of the oars and whacked Billy on the shin with it. He gave a loud yelp and started hopping around, holding his leg.

'You crazy fucking retard,' he was shouting. 'Now I'm definitely telling. About you stealing and you hitting me. My dad's going to have you put in jail.'

I hit him on the other shin and he fell onto the ground and rolled up in a ball, clutching both knees close to his chest. He was trying to say something but there was only a kind of squealing noise coming out of his lips. Then I pushed the boat the rest of the way into the water and started rowing as fast as I could.

*

Out on the river the current carried me quickly downstream. The melt water had swelled it after the thaw and it was still running strong. After a while I hardly needed to use the oars at all, except for steering, and in a few minutes the town was behind me.

In some places dead trees and branches had got snagged in the middle of the current, and when I swerved to avoid them I could see the reeds and rushes unfolding themselves and getting their colour back after all the months frozen in the snow and ice, and below me, in the shallows, the long underwater weeds called mermaid's hair because they looked like hair blowing in a breeze. It seemed like a long time since I'd first come this way with George. Sometimes the shore would seem familiar and then I'd look again and it wouldn't. Sometimes I'd steer the boat in towards the bank, thinking I'd reached the spot, but it'd turn out to be just another bed of reeds and rushes and outcrops of rock; and then, in front of me, a bend in the river would appear and I'd think I recognized it from before. In the end I was lucky. I spotted a little piece of orange in the trees. George's marker was still hanging from the branch he'd put it on.

Making my way over the outcrop of rock and into the woods, I kept expecting to see George. I reckoned he'd probably be out exploring or something. I called out his name a few times but there wasn't any reply.

In the clearing it was still and quiet. The only sounds were the cawing of some ravens, hopping from branch to branch above me. Watching them I noticed how the clearing had been cut real carefully: it was only the smaller trees that'd been cleared – the taller ones, with the longest branches, had been left standing. You would've never been able to spot it from above. Someone had covered the whole mound with dead brush so it looked just the same as a pile of blow-down. If you didn't know it was there you'd probably never have found it. When I went to check I found the bear trap still there and still set, with its teeth gone all rusty like old pine needles.

I called out George's name and again there wasn't any answer. There were no signs of anything anywhere. No footprints or nothing. The place where the door used to be was hidden beneath the brush and when I cleared it I found a big rock there instead. It was then I began thinking I'd made a mistake.

I checked a second time for signs, more closely this time. If there'd been footprints then somebody must've rubbed them or something because I couldn't find them. Or not recent ones, anyhow. There were a few marks in the moss and pine needles but they could've been anything. If George was here he would've been stomping around everywhere. I would've seen something. I would've known. Sitting down on the moss I tried thinking hard, like one of George's detectives, while the ravens kept up their cawing above me as if they reckoned I was too stupid to figure anything out. I felt mad at myself for being dumb and it got hard to breathe, like the cord was around my neck again. Nobody was here. Nobody had been here for a while. It didn't make any sense to me. My thoughts were like the ravens' calls – hoarse and ragged and teasing.

And then I had an idea.

If Mr McKenzie was in his house then maybe George was too? Maybe he was just hiding him so he couldn't go back to school or live at Gracie's. It suddenly made sense. That was why Mr McKenzie wasn't here. That was why he'd built his fence so high and everything. To hide George. I got up then to go. I was going to tell Virgil and Gracie and everybody. I was going to tell them I'd figured it all out and I wouldn't have to say about the underground place or nothing. I wouldn't be breaking any promise. As I was leaving I stopped for a second to throw some pine cones at the ravens. See, I shouted at them. I figured it. I figured it out on my own. They flew off pretty quick.

And it was then I heard it.

It was hardly anything. It was a tiny scratching, scrabbling noise, the same as a squirrel makes when it runs across a roof. If it hadn't been so quiet in the clearing I would never have heard it. I listened for it again.

It was coming from behind me. Turning around, I began walking back towards the mound and could hear it clearer. Scratch, scratch, scrape, scrape. It was getting louder and more frantic. I followed it. It was coming from under the big rock.

'George,' I shouted.

It got louder and louder.

It took all my strength to move the rock. I wrapped my arms around it and pulled and pulled until the sweat was dripping into my eyes and I'd finally moved it clear of the wooden door beneath.

At first, after I'd opened the door, I could hardly see nothing on account of the sweat in my eyes, just a blurry dark square beneath my feet. A draught of damp, musty air rose up and crept into my nostrils; it smelt stale and stinky like the inside of an old outhouse. And then a white, watery circle appeared in the dark square. I rubbed my sleeve over my eyes. There was George's face, staring up at me. His eyes were wide, pink discs.

'I heard you shouting,' he whimpered. 'But I thought you were dead. I thought everyone was dead. He left me here. He said everyone was dead and he left me down here. I couldn't get out. I couldn't get out.'

When he reached up to me from the steps I could see the blood on his fingernails from where he'd been scratching at the door.

Outside in the clearing George leaned against a tree for a while, blinking and taking quick, short gulps of breath, like he was tasting the air, like he didn't trust it enough to take a long deep breath. He kept saying:

'I couldn't get out. I . . . couldn't g . . . g . . . get *out*.'

But after a bit he managed to get enough air inside him and told me what'd happened.

He said his dad and him had set out early in the morning, when it was still dark, and almost as soon as they'd arrived his dad had said he had to go back to fetch the final batch of supplies. As he was leaving he told George that the end of the world might happen any moment now – it was imminent – and he was going to tell Gracie everything, including about how they'd prepared a safe place. He said he was going to bring her back with him so they could all live together again. He said she'd understand everything then, and why things had got difficult like they did. She'd be real pleased that George and him had been smart enough to have made preparations. But it was very important that George didn't leave the bunker, not even for a second. He said there might be poison in the air. Fallout. He had a special mask to protect himself, but only the one, and if George breathed the poison then he'd probably get sick, so sick there'd be nothing they could do.

George said to begin with it was OK. He thought it'd only be a few hours. He waited and waited, reading some magazines and comics he'd brought with him, using the light of the flashlight. He'd wished he'd brought a watch then, because there wasn't a clock in the bunker and after a while he didn't know how much time had gone by. It felt like a lot but he didn't know. He waited and waited. He fell asleep and when he woke up he didn't know whether he'd been sleeping for hours or minutes or seconds. He tried counting the seconds, to keep track of how much time was going by, but that just made him fall asleep again and when he woke up it was worse. He didn't even know if was daytime or night-time. It felt like he could have been waiting for an hour or ten hours or a hundred hours – he didn't know any more, he didn't know what an hour felt like any more.

And then his dad had come back. When the door opened he could see it was dark so he thought it was the next night or something. His dad never said how long he'd been gone for. Gracie wasn't with him.

When George asked where she was Mr McKenzie told him things were terrible out there. Everything had happened just like he'd said it would. The poison was falling from the sky and everybody in town had got sick with it. They wouldn't make it, he said. From now on it was just them. 'We have to concentrate on our own survival now,' he told George.

'But what about mum?' George asked.

'Oh . . . she's fine,' Mr McKenzie told him. 'She's just packing a few last things.'

'But what about the poison?'

'That's not a problem. She's got my mask.'

'What about you?'

'I found another one.'

'Where is it?'

'It's outside. Look George, it's vital we concentrate on the important things right now.'

Mr McKenzie told George that the most important thing was that he didn't go outside, not even for a second. The poison was falling everywhere. The only reason he'd come now was to check George hadn't and warn him. He said he had to go straight back to town to collect Gracie. She'd probably be finished her packing any moment. And then he was gone.

The waiting started again, except it was much worse this time because the batteries in the flashlight died and he couldn't find new ones because it was too dark – it was pitch black. He didn't bother trying to count or nothing this time. When he was tired he slept and when he was hungry he fumbled around in the darkness until he found a can. He never knew what was inside the cans till he tasted it. His dad had left a bucket in the corner for him to do his business in and it started to smell real bad. Then he knocked it over in the darkness and it smelt even worse.

Inside the bunker it was damp and cold and once he started shivering he couldn't stop. And he'd begun hearing things.

At first he thought they were voices calling for him. He thought he heard his dad. He thought he heard his mum. He called back and waited. And waited. Nothing happened. The voices went away. When they came back he listened more carefully. It was only sometimes they sounded like voices – other times they just sounded like owls or ravens or animals. He stopped calling back then and even when they did sound like voices he didn't believe in them any more.

It was around then that George decided he was going to go out, just for a second, just to peek, just to see. The poison didn't seem as bad as the darkness and the shivering and the smell. He said the underground place felt like it was getting smaller and smaller around him, like it was shrinking – he felt like he could hardly move, he felt like he could hardly breathe. He'd wrap one of his T-shirts over his mouth just in case.

The door wouldn't open. He pushed it again. It wouldn't budge. George took a deep breath and sat down on the steps to think. What was wrong? Why wouldn't the door open? What would an explorer do about a door that wouldn't open? But the only thing he could think was, I must get it open. *I must get it open. I can't breathe. I can't move. I can't get out.* He pushed and pushed until he didn't have any strength left and then he started scraping and scratching at the door like an animal. He was scraping and scratching and outside he could hear the voices again and this time they sounded like me. But he knew it couldn't be me. Because of the poison. Because of the fallout. And then the door had started opening and he'd taken a few steps back down. Then he saw me but for a second or two he didn't believe it.

I told George that nothing had happened: it wasn't the end of the world and there was no poison falling. Gracie and everyone was fine. The only thing that'd happened was him going missing and everyone looking for him.

'How long?' he asked. I looked at him. His eyes were still blinking in the light. They were pinker then I'd ever seen them. His skin and hair were as white as the melted snow.

'How many days?' he said. 'How many days have I been down there?'

'This is the fourth,' I said. 'It's Sunday.'

'Where's my dad?'

'He's at your house.'

George started looking around him then – at the trees and the ground and the sky – as if he'd only just noticed they were still there. He took a long, deep gulp of air.

'He was lying,' he said. 'He lied to me.'

George and me were about halfway back to the boat when we spotted the canoe coming down the river. We ducked behind the outcrop of rock and watched it. I thought maybe it was one of the search parties. Or Buddy come to find his boat: Billy had seen me take it; he'd probably told everybody already.

'It's him,' George whispered.

I looked again. It was Mr McKenzie.

George crept slowly back from the outcrop, staying on his hands and knees.

'Come on,' he hissed.

'Where you going?' I asked.

'We've got to get out of here,' he said. His face was set hard in fright. 'He'll make me go back in there, Eli. He lied to me. He'll make me go back and I won't go. I won't.'

He'd made it to the edge of the trees and I followed him, staying low and keeping behind the outcrop.

'Where shall we go?' I whispered.

'I don't care,' George said. 'Anywhere.'

When we were both in the cover of the trees we started running. We ran and we ran. We tripped over blow-down and rocks and roots. Branches hit our faces. But we never stopped. We ran and we ran until at last our breath ran out.

We were by the side of a creek that ran into a wide swamp. Following the creek, we came to a bunch of high cattails and pushed our way into them. It was like being in a cocoon or something. We waited there for a long time, getting our breath back, listening, not saying a word.

'I don't think he's following us,' George said at last.

'He'd never find us in here,' I said.

We waited some more, though, just to make sure.

'Where do you reckon we are, then?' I asked.

'I don't know,' George said.

'I reckon we're lost.'

'I think you're right,' George said.

And I could've sworn then I saw the ghost of a smile beginning to shape his lips. He peeked out of the reeds.

'I've never been here before,' he said. 'Not ever.'

X Marks the Spot

'There's no need for that, you know,' Buddy said from over the fence.

I was pulling up the rotten boards from the porch and piling them in the garden. I'd already taken out the old screens and bought some new ones.

'There's really no need. I never said anything about you not staying on at the Poplars. I never said anything about that, Eli. You're welcome to stay on there. I don't like this business any more than you do.'

'I'm just fixing it up,' I said. 'It's not so bad. It just needs some work.'

'It needs a lot of work, Eli. A hell of a lot. It's not fit to live in.'

'I can fix it,' I said. I didn't want to tell Buddy, but I'd had an idea I hadn't told anyone about yet. I'd had it after talking to Sarah the day before and I'd come right into town to get started.

'Look,' said Buddy. 'I'm just on my way to check something out. Why don't you come along with me?'

*

Buddy and me drove out through town, bumping along Main until we passed the museum, and then towards the Red Rock road. Buddy was looking out his side window at the houses. There was a big frown on his face.

'Will you look at this place now?' he said. 'I remember clear as day when every house round here was brand new. We had them built for the mine workers. Every one of them new. And look at them now – half of them empty and falling down and the other half as good as. They might as well pull the whole bunch down and be done with it. It's a real eyesore.'

Buddy's one of those wiry old guys who reach a certain age and then you don't know how old they are – they sort of stay put, not changing. He looks pretty much the same as always, even though he must be well into his eighties. But as he peered out the truck window he seemed older suddenly, as if looking at the rundown houses made him seem like them. I noticed how hunched he was over the steering wheel and the brown spots covering his hands.

We parked up alongside the southern edge of the pit and while Buddy was getting out I walked towards the old beach. Straight away I could see the water there below me – shining and glistening, a small lake in the bottom of the pit. Across to my right the trickle of water had become a waterfall, cascading down over the edge.

'Well, I'll be damned,' said Buddy from behind me. 'I'll be goddamned.' When I turned around his face had gone kind of slow and wizened and blinking, like a turtle's.

We walked a little further, until we came to the sand of the old beach. Buddy asked me to give him a hand to sit.

His legs were weak and wobbly as I lowered him onto the sand. I sat down beside him and together we watched the waterfall tumbling into the pit, throwing up foam and mist where it fell into the water beneath.

'They said what'd happened,' he said quietly. 'I suppose I just didn't expect it to happen this quick.'

Neither of us said anything for a while then.

'Do you know what a legacy is, Eli?' Buddy asked me. 'Well, I guess this is what I thought mine would be. Hundreds of people used to work down there. I thought I'd made something that would last, that people would always remember. Forget all that junk at the museum and the Poplars. Forget the bait store and the outfitters and all that. Forget all of that stuff. *This* was it. *This* was the thing.'

'They used to have picnics here,' I said.

'What?'

'Before you came here,' I said. 'When it was still a lake. And afterwards my grandfather used to play the fiddle in the hotel.'

'I never saw him play,' Buddy said. 'You know, me and your grandfather had a lot in common, Eli. We both came here with nothing. We came here to make something of ourselves. And we both married late . . . maybe too late. We were busy men. We had a lot to prove and this was a tough place to prove it.'

Beneath us you could see the water lapping against the red stone and earth of the pit. Soon it'd reach the dark seams of granite.

'Look, Eli, I'm sorry about all this business with Billy.

He's a hothead and he doesn't listen to me any more. I guess some of that's my own fault – I always gave him whatever he wanted and I suppose he got to expecting it. He never had to work at things like I did. But I don't want you thinking you have to move out of the Poplars – you're welcome to stay there as long as you want, as long as it's still standing. I mean, Jesus, your family's been unlucky enough as it is.'

He meant what with Clarence, and then Mum and Dad, and then Virgil getting sick. People weren't meant to get sick that young. That's what everyone said at the time. It wasn't meant to happen to a man in his prime like that. It was just bad stupid luck. And people couldn't even look at me and Nana properly then, as if the bad stupid luck had been sprinkled on me and my family like germs, like it was contagious somehow. I remember Virgil thin and frail and hurting, saying for me to look after my Nana, saying not to remember him like this, saying don't look back. And I always tried not to, just like he said. And I did look after Nana too, for those last years, just like he said. And afterwards when I thought about them it was like following Clarence's footsteps down to the river: when I reached a certain point they'd disappear and I wouldn't be able to follow them any further. But I wouldn't be able to follow them back either, and the river would flow around and around in a loop, in a circle.

'. . . I'm not asking you for anything, Eli,' Buddy said. 'I'm only saying maybe you should give Billy a bit of a wide berth for a while. Until he's off the warpath.'

I helped Buddy up from the sand and we walked back

together towards the truck. Before we got there Buddy took one last look behind him.

'Christ,' he said. 'The whole place will be a lake again in a couple of days.'

'I reckon most water is like a dog . . .' I started saying. But he wasn't listening.

On the way back to town I got Buddy to drop me off at the road to the Poplars. I couldn't wait to tell Sarah and Bobby about my idea and I was running down the road so I could find them when I reached the entrance to the Poplars and nearly slammed straight into Billy's truck. It was coming at me so quick I hardly had time to jump to the side. Billy veered at the last moment and went into the ditch. Bobby was sitting beside him in the front seat. His seatbelt was pulled tight across his chest and his face was pale with fright.

'For fuck's sake,' Billy said, climbing out the door and stepping into the ditch. '*Eli!* I should've known. I should've just carried straight on.' He was shaking his head and looking down at the bumper.

'If you've damaged this truck . . .' he was saying.

'Where's Sarah?' I asked.

'Oh, what . . . ? So you're worried about your *girlfriend* now, are you? Isn't that fucking sweet? Well, no need to wet yourself, Eli. She's back there in the Pine dorm. Packing up her things, I hope. She's all fucking yours.'

'Where you taking Bobby?'

'That's none of your frigging business.'

'Where you taking him?'

'Do you really want to know, Eli? Do you? Let me fill you in, then. I'll spell it out nice and slow for you so you can understand it. I'm not too keen on my kid living out here in the boonies with a slut and a retard. Do you get that? Is that simple enough for you? I'm taking him back to a decent home.'

'He doesn't want to go with you,' I said. 'Sarah says you can't take him.'

'Oh, really? Well, this really is a turn-up for the books. Eli O'Callaghan telling me what I can and can't do with my kid. Eli O'Callaghan giving me advice on family matters. Let me just see. Let me just have a little flick through the old O'Callaghan family tree. What a success story *that* was. Grandfather goes AWOL; dad tops himself; son an idiot; uncle . . .'

'Don't talk about them.'

'Talk about happy fucking families . . .'

'I *said* don't talk about them.'

'What an almighty train wreck . . . Good thing your mum . . .'

I couldn't feel my fist when it hit Billy in the face. It was like it was someone else's fist. And I was someone else watching it happen. And then we were down in the water of the ditch. Sometimes I was under the water and sometimes Billy was. And then just Billy was and I was pressing his head into the mud until finally he stopped moving and I could feel my hands pressing down on his head. That's when I stopped. For a while Billy just lay there as if he was asleep in the water.

I went to turn him over and when I did his chest suddenly started heaving up and down. A big spout of muddy water came rushing up from his mouth, like out of a whale's back, and then he started coughing up more of it, brown at first and then kind of green. When he'd finished, he sat up and looked around him for a long time. His eyes seemed like they couldn't focus properly, but when they could again he pointed them right at me.

'You tried to kill me,' he said. 'You tried to fucking kill me. You're going to pay for this, Eli. They're going to lock you up.'

I looked over at the truck and Billy's eyes followed mine. The cab was empty. Bobby was gone.

'You tried to kill me . . . you fucking lunatic. I'm going to the police,' Billy said.

I went to find Bobby.

The door to the Pine dorm was locked. I knocked on it a few times but nobody answered. When I went around to the back I found Sarah climbing out a window.

'Eli,' she said. 'Is that you, Eli?' She sounded all frantic. Her head and shoulders were out of the window but the rest of her was stuck in the frame. 'Get me out of here,' she said. '*PLEASE*. GET ME OUT OF HERE!' Her eyes were black and mad again, like the owl's.

'That fucking prick,' she said when I got her out. 'He locked me in there, that fucking prick. Where is he? Where is he, Eli? Don't tell me he's taken him.'

I said how I'd almost bumped into them in the truck,

how the truck had gone into the ditch, how Billy had gone back into town on foot.

'So where is he then, Eli? Where's Bobby?'

'I don't know,' I said.

'What do you mean, you don't know?'

'I don't know,' I said. 'I don't know where he is.'

Sarah and me checked all the dorms and the office and everywhere. She shouted his name into the woods but there wasn't any answer. I went through them a couple of hundred yards to look for signs but I couldn't find any. The sun was beginning to fall when she phoned the police. We waited for them outside the office. Sarah sat on the steps beside Buddy's sculpture. Her head was in her hands.

'Oh God,' she said. 'Oh God, oh God,' she kept saying.

It didn't take long for Officer Red to arrive in his car. He spoke to Sarah for a while and wrote down what she said in his book. He asked me what'd happened with Billy and the truck and I told him. Then he went to speak on his radio and when he came back he said there wasn't much they could do right now because it was so late and there wasn't enough light left. But don't worry, he told Sarah, they'd have search parties ready first thing in the morning. They'd have a helicopter too and they'd be out there at first light. And maybe Bobby would be back by then anyway. That was what he hoped. That's what often happened in these circumstances – in his experience. Stay put here, he said. And if anything happened, contact him immediately. He'd be in touch as soon as it was light tomorrow.

As he was walking back to his car he beckoned me over. 'Can I have a quick word, Eli?' he asked.

Over by the car he whispered, 'Look, Eli, I know this is a bad time but there's something I wanted to tell you.'

'About Billy?' I said.

'No, not about Billy. We've already had him down at the station blabbing about how he was almost murdered. But I know the situation. It sounded like a fair fight to me. You didn't do anything wrong, Eli. This isn't your fault. We'll find him . . . Bobby, I mean. It's important you tell her that. We'll find him. No, this isn't about that. It's about your grandfather.'

'The remains,' I said.

'Yes,' he said. 'It's about the remains.'

I didn't say nothing.

'We've had the tests back.'

I still didn't say nothing.

'I don't know quite how to say this . . . but they didn't match. It's not him, Eli. I'm sorry.'

He got into the car then, but as he started the engine he opened the window.

'Tell her not to worry,' he said again. 'We're going to do everything we can. In my experience ninety-nine times out of a hundred . . .'

But I didn't hear the rest. All I could hear was a sound like water rushing around and around in my head.

As soon as he'd gone, with the sun dipping towards the top of the second island, I set out along the eastern shore of Eye Lake to find Bobby. I had no plan. I had no map. I couldn't see any signs. I was just going to walk and walk until I found him.

I followed the shoreline to begin with. Or at least what had used to be the shoreline. The water level had dropped a long way – so far you could see the muddy bed of the lake for twenty or thirty feet in places, covered in piles of weed shrivelling in the air. The underwater trees were poking above the surface everywhere, like they were growing out of the water, and the ones that had always stuck up out of the surface were getting taller and taller. It was like seeing a new forest appear – a forest with no leaves except the slime and weeds that hung from slippery, stunted branches. As the sun touched the horizon it turned the mud a shining red and pink, and its light fell through the new forest, turning it that bright golden-green that was the colour of fevers.

Places where I'd fished once were in the open air now. Rock beds and outcrops and sandbars, which I'd only known were down there from snags and lost lures, were in front of my eyes. Everything had changed. Everything looked different. As the light began to fail it threw the second island into silhouette and I could see it was turning back into a hill. Reefs that I'd once trolled around were turning back into ridges.

It was nearly dark when I reached the castle. I could see the black shape of the tower and the sloping roof and the whole of the second and third storeys. It was bigger than I'd ever thought. Out beyond it, about a hundred yards into the lake, you could see the river flowing. Its current blackly rippled the skin of the water like the backs of surfacing fish.

I could've walked most of the way to the castle if I'd wanted to. The mud stretched out from the place I'd first cast with the phantom shad. But in the near dark I couldn't help thinking about the watchers. Where would they be now the waters were falling so fast? I imagined their eyes opening to find the night sky clear above them, blinking in the air, flashing like the lights of fireflies on the bed of the emptying lake. That did it for me, and I headed into the bush, behind the cover of the trees.

Beneath the branches there was no light at all. I got turned around pretty fast and didn't know what direction I was moving in. The lower branches scraped against my face and my feet stumbled over rocks and roots and blow-down. There were noises all around me: the calling of loons and the hooting of owls and then other sounds from animals I couldn't tell properly – shrieks and howls and snapping twigs. I don't know how long I spent wandering in there, or how far I'd gone, but eventually I began to hear another noise that didn't sound like any animal at all. It was a low whispering noise, like lots of voices speaking at once, and it seemed to come from all around me. At first I tried to walk away from it but whatever direction I took I just seemed to get closer and closer and it got louder and louder.

'Bobby.' I tried to shout, but my own voice came out weak and small and dry like there was no air in my lungs or spit in my mouth.

'Bobby.' The whispering got louder and louder.

A white, silvery light appeared ahead of me. It seemed to move this way and that, flickering, catching on the black bark of branches and tree trunks. Sometimes I'd think it was in one place but then I'd lose sight of it and it'd appear again in another. I couldn't tell whether I was following it or it was following me. Closing my eyes I started to run. I ran blind.

I don't know how long I was down for. My feet were tangled in some roots and my face was pressed into the moss and pine needles. As I lifted it I could sense an emptiness in front of me where the trees had thinned out into a clearing. The noise was loud. It was right beside me. And the light was there too. Dancing and flickering. It was the light of the moon shining down on running water. I knew where I was then. I was lying on the bank of the Crooked River.

I realized that in the dark I must've headed north, up to where the river came into Eye Lake. I must've been going in circles through the bush because I hadn't reached far: the castle was only a few hundred yards down the shore from where the river joined the lake.

Sitting up, I looked around me, and in the silvery light from the moon I could see the twisted branches of an old red pine leaning across the river towards an outcrop of rock on the opposite bank, as if it was pointing to it with long gnarled fingers.

If it had been daytime, and if the light had been stronger, then I would've been able to see the small, faint X scraped into the black lichen covering the face of the rock. Virgil had scraped it there forty years before. It was to mark the spot opposite where Clarence went missing. It was in the bare dirt beneath the red pine's branches that they'd found his last footprints. They'd gone down to the edge of the river. And then they'd disappeared.

The Blue Danube

Virgil and Dad used to tell a story about the last visitors who stayed at the Pioneer Hotel. They were two fishermen from Minnesota, and they arrived in town one day on the new highway. It was about ten years after the war. Dad was around twelve and Virgil was a year younger.

The men arrived in a big new car and parked right outside the front door of the hotel. The sign still hung outside it back then. Dad and Virgil were playing in the porch of number one O'Callaghan Street and they came out onto the pavement to get a better look at the car. It was a Chevy Bel Air. When the men got out they eyed the hotel suspiciously for a long while. One of them started scratching his beard.

It wasn't such a promising sight in those days, they said. There was almost no paint left on the walls and the wood was all weathered and warped. The front steps sagged in the middle, and up above the stone chimney had started to lean like the tower of Pisa. There were boards nailed across some of the windows on the second floor.

'Is this place open for business?' one of the men asked Virgil.

'Sure,' he said. 'I guess.' They hadn't had actual visitors in a while. 'I'll go fetch my dad.'

When Clarence let them in they started looking even more suspicious. There was a perfect carpet of dust covering the surface of the reception desk and a family of spiders had moved into the cubbyholes where the room keys were kept – each one had a cosy little nest to itself.

'Are you sure this place is open for business?' one of the men asked Clarence.

'It is now,' he said.

'What's our room number?' the other man asked.

Clarence handed him the master key. 'I'll tell you what, you go ahead and pick whatever one you like.'

That night, as they sat out on the porch, Virgil and Dad listened to the noises coming from next door. They could hear banging and crashing and the sound of feet stomping across the rickety floorboards. Sometimes it'd go quiet for a half-hour or so and then it'd start on up again.

First thing the next morning, as soon as it began to get light, there was a loud knock on the front door of number one O'Callaghan Street. When Clarence opened it the two fishermen were standing there, with white faces and bags the size of flour sacks under their eyes.

'Jesus,' the first one said. 'You never said about the bugs in there. I don't reckon I know if there were more mosquitoes above me or bedbugs beneath me.'

'Or the mice,' said the second one. 'I've never seen mice that big before. I spent half the night checking my toes were still there.'

'Or them bats,' said the first one. 'I've never seen flocks of bats before.'

'Or them squirrels . . .' said the second one.

'Squirrels?' Clarence said.

'I swear there were more of them under my bed than there are living in the woods.'

'Squirrels,' said Clarence. 'Well, I didn't know there were squirrels in there. I guess I'll have to charge extra for them.'

It wasn't so long after that they took the hotel sign down.

The Pioneer Hotel still wasn't totally closed for business, though. Clarence kept the bar open in the dining room. You could reach it through a door at the side, Virgil and Dad told me, and it became pretty popular with men who didn't much mind about their surroundings when they drank. There were a bunch of men working out at the mine by then and most of them weren't too fussy.

When they remembered Clarence, Virgil and Dad mostly remembered him from this time. Sometimes he let them help out at the bar, carrying bottles of beer over to the men sitting at the long wooden table. The men played cards and talked. Sometimes Clarence joined them for a hand or two. When they got to talking he just listened, mostly. He wasn't a big talker, so they said.

If Jim or Jake or another of the old-timers was in they'd tell stories about the early days of Crooked River. They made those days sound like the Wild West – kind of tough and new and free and full of adventures. Virgil and Dad used to hang on every word they said, but Clarence would sort of just drift away – as if there was always something needed fetching or doing – even though a lot of the time he was in those stories. 'I remember when your dad . . .' the old-timers would tell them. And afterwards Virgil and Dad wouldn't be able to quite fit what they'd heard with the dad they knew.

There used to be a little path worn into the garden between number one O'Callaghan Street and the pile of boards left over from the Pioneer Hotel. It was still there when I was a kid. The earth was rubbed smooth and the grass hadn't grown back on it yet. It was made by Clarence walking back and forth every day to the hotel. That's what he did mostly by then.

And that was how Virgil and Dad saw him, mostly. Not as a Crooked River pioneer in those Wild West times, but just a quiet old man who walked back and forth to the hotel every day and afterwards sat on the porch and played cribbage with Nana.

Virgil and Dad weren't helping out in the bar two years later on the night Walt Mathison's uncle came to the hotel; Virgil didn't hear about that night until one of the evenings on the porch talking to Jim.

Walt's uncle was up visiting from Minneapolis for the week and had been fishing out on the floodwaters for a few days. There was only Jim and Jake in that night. They were playing cards with Clarence when Walt arrived, with his uncle in tow. They introduced themselves and dealt him in.

Jim told Virgil they just talked fishing the first few hands – Walt's uncle was real pleased to have caught some big slubes. And then the conversation began to wander.

Me and Jake got to remembering the wolf man, Jim said. We asked Walt's uncle if he might have heard about him – him being from Minneapolis and of a similar age and everything. I'm not so sure I ever did hear of him, he said. It's a big place. And besides, he wasn't living there back then, he said. He was living in Chicago. That's where he was raised.

He was interested in the story, though, and so we filled him in. And then naturally we went on to the day of the picnic and the circus man from Chicago, Jim said. We must have told pretty much the whole story – about the wolf man and the bear, about the man and woman reminiscing about their lost place on the banks of the Danube – before Walt's uncle's ears started perking up. On the Danube? he said. A circus, you say?

He said there were lots of circuses in Chicago back in those days. But he remembered going to one in particular. It had a dancing bear and he'd gone to see it. Its owner was a sharp-looking guy from the west side of the city. Or at least that's where Walt's uncle thought he was from: he'd heard him talking to some fellows outside his tent before he went in and the man definitely sounded like he was from the west side. He only started sounding different when he was in the tent. He looked different too.

He'd changed out of his suit into some kind of colourful silk pyjamas and was wearing a big fur hat. He introduced himself as Ivor in a deep booming foreign voice. He was holding a tambourine. After a few shakes he said he'd like to introduce everybody to one of the wonders of the animal kingdom, a bona fide artist in fur, brought up on the Steppes and rescued from the very palace of the Russian Tsar. He'd performed in front of all the greatest lords and ladies of Europe, his name was fabled from the Volga to the Thames, but now it was Chicago's great good fortune to be able to witness him in the flesh.

'May I present,' he boomed, reaching into a cage at the back of the tent draped in a white sheet . . . 'May I present Misha?'

There was a piece of rope in his hand and after he gave it a few sharp tugs out came this little black bear. He was wearing a conical hat with a tassel on top and a multicoloured waistcoat. The rope was attached through a hole in his nose. He looked miserable.

'Misha,' boomed the man. 'Let us show our audience the polka.'

With one hand he shook the tambourine and with the other he tugged the rope. The bear let out a sad bellow, stood up, and started shuffling slowly from foot to foot.

'And now the Barynya.' He tugged the rope harder and the bear swayed and shuffled a bit faster, as though the floor was made of hot coals.

It wasn't much to look at, Walt's uncle said. It was pretty much the most miserable bear he'd ever seen. If he hadn't already paid his nickel he would've left.

As the performance came to an end, and the bear crawled back into his cage, the man turned to the audience and said with a big wink, 'And for those gentlemen in the audience who are aficionados of the dance, might I recommend some of the entertainments provided for your perusal off the midway.' It was the kind of invitation no fifteen-year-old boy needed to hear twice, Walt's uncle said.

Off the midway there were freaks and fortune-tellers and 'Exhibitions of the Strange and Miraculous'. And further along, on the very shadiest, shiftiest edges of the circus, where the men had their hats pulled down and their collars pulled up, were tents with smaller signs outside them that you had to crane your neck to read. Cleopatra and the Asp. The Dance of the Seven Veils. Lady Godiva Comes To Town. And there was one in particular that took Walt's uncle's eye. Princess Ludovika performs The Blue Danube, it announced.

After paying his quarter Walt's uncle went and stood in the tent. There were a handful of men in front of him, waiting with their hands in their pockets, but he managed to worm his way past them to the front. There was a piece of red string separating the floor from the stage, which was made of wooden boxes pressed together with a big carpet spread across them; the colours and patterns on it had faded and it was worn and threadbare in patches. Above the stage hung a cheap glass chandelier, and behind it, draped across the whole back of the tent, was a panorama painted on canvas.

It wasn't no Leanardo da Vinci, he told us. But it wasn't half bad. On one side there was a castle, with high *walls of white stone and columns and arched windows and doors, and brightly coloured flags hanging from its turrets. And in front of the castle, sweeping across the back of the tent, were deep green lawns, dotted with stately old trees and flower beds and marble fountains full of mermaids. These gardens swept right to the other end of the panorama, where they reached the banks of a painted blue river which meandered away into the distance, towards a rising full moon, before flowing off the edge of the canvas. It wasn't half bad at all, he said, though some of the flowers had turned a bit brown where someone had spilt beer on them, and there was a piece of hotdog smeared on the tail of one of the mermaids.*

They waited for a few minutes, the air filling up with tobacco smoke and the smell of beery breath, until finally a thin opening at the side of the tent slowly parted. A hand appeared. A slender white arm. And there she was, Princess Ludovika herself. And she was dressed just like a princess too, Walt's uncle said. She was wearing a long flowing ball gown, made of satin and lace. It made a soft, swishing sound as she walked over to the other side of the stage, where, without saying a word, she put a record on an old gramophone that was sitting on a table there and began winding it.

It was pretty scratchy at first, but soon enough the sound of a waltz started up and Princess Ludovika began to sway and swirl in time with it. She moved in elegant circles around the stage, her arms stretched out before her as if she were holding an invisible partner. Her eyes were half-closed like she was all dreamily lost in the music, and from below the stage it looked as if her feet were dancing on the deep green of the castle lawns. She moved so gracefully you hardly noticed her clothes coming off. They just slipped away like petals in a breeze – the satin dress and the petticoats and the corsets, all of them – without her ever missing a step. And she carried on dancing right to the end of the waltz, as if she hadn't even noticed she was naked herself. It was only when the record came to a stop that she opened her eyes properly and seemed to notice us all watching her. She reached down then to get hold of her gown and wrapped herself in it. And then, without a word, she slipped back out the side of the tent.

As Walt's uncle had finished this story, he'd smiled to himself. *Ah yes,* The Blue Danube, *he'd said. I certainly remember that.*

And what about Clarence? Virgil asked Jim. What was he doing when Walt's uncle was telling all this?

He just carried on playing his cards, Jim said. We were playing rummy but we could've been playing poker, the way he kept his face. Not a twitch. Not a flicker. He carried right on till the end of the hand and then stood up slowly and said, 'Right, gentlemen, I'm going to have to call it a night, I'm afraid. You can lock up yourselves when you're done.'

You know that was the night before, Virgil said. The night before he—

I know, Jim said. That was the very last time I saw him.

*

Virgil told Jim he'd been awake when Clarence came back that night. He was in the kitchen having a glass of milk and watched him walk back across the garden as usual. And as usual he sat down in his chair on the porch and started a hand of cribbage with Nana. He was halfway through counting a hand – two fives and two jacks – when he mentioned to her he'd be heading off fishing in the morning. It'll be real early, he told her. I've got a new spot I want to try. Don't fuss about getting up yourself, he said.

Virgil said he didn't know exactly why he woke up so early the next day himself. But it was barely light when he did, and he just lay there in bed staring out the window, trying to get back to sleep. He could hear someone shuffling quietly about in the kitchen and then the faint click of the porch door, and then he watched Clarence go by below him on the sidewalk, wearing an old black jacket full of holes, his slow, steady steps hardly making a sound, moving through the half-dark of the morning until he reached the corner and turned and disappeared.

There was something not quite right, Virgil said. And I couldn't for the life of me put a finger on it at the time. I fell back to sleep and it wasn't till I woke up again and the sun was properly up that I figured out what it was. He hadn't been carrying his fishing rod. He hadn't been carrying anything.

And that was the very last time I saw him, Virgil said.

They didn't ever find a body, not a single bone. They had nothing to place into the earth and put a stone over. And so Clarence's only remains were these last things: his last words and conversations; the last place he'd been seen; the last plans he'd made. Ordinary things you'd take no notice of usually but that somehow got fixed in people's minds because they were the last, like they were prints made in air and time, just the same as the prints his feet had made in the dirt.

The Lost Highway

George said we should head north. I said we should head east. If we hit the river then it'd be easy enough to find our way back to town – that was our thinking – but neither of us knew for certain what direction the river was in any more. To be honest, neither of us knew where north or east was neither. The only difference was that George thought he did know.

Look at this moss here, he'd say, rooting about in the woods. It's growing much thicker on this side of the trunks. Look at these flowers coming through. Look at the sun. It's *obvious*. That way's north. George was really liking this being lost, you could tell. He seemed to have forgotten all about the underground place. He was so excited he was jumping around like a jack.

'But I reckon that way's east.'

'Eli, Eli,' he said. 'Who's seen the most maps of here? Who's studied them?'

'I don't care about no maps. I think it's east. It felt like we were heading west when we started running.'

'It *felt* like we were heading west? How do you *feel* a direction, Eli? That's dumb. I remember seeing maps of around here showing a swamp and a creek like this to the south of the shelter.'

'There's a hundred swamps and creeks around here,' I said. 'There's hundreds of them. How'd you know for sure it was these ones?'

But it was no use arguing with George. He had an answer for everything. And besides it was getting on and I reckoned any direction was better than none, even if neither of us knew for certain what direction it really was.

We set off into the bush.

'After a full and frank discussion about their bearings,' George said, 'they decided on a northerly course.'

It was pretty tough going at first. The ground was wet and swampy and sometimes our feet would sink through the surface right up to our knees. It wasn't too warm down there neither. And when we eventually made it onto the higher ground of a ridge, the blow-down was so thick it took us a while to creep our way through it.

When we reached the top of the ridge we stopped to get a view of the land around us. In every direction there were more trees and more swamps and more ridges. The river was nowhere in sight.

By then our clothes were already in a bad way. Both our shirts had tears in them and our shoes and pants were soaking. There was a big scrape on George's cheek where a branch had hit him. We sat down on a rock for a bit and I stared around us at the trees and swamps and ridges, beginning to feel sorry for myself. But George seemed about as pleased as could be. He was peering in front of him with his hand held up to his forehead to keep the sun out of his eyes.

'I think our best route is that way,' he said, pointing ahead. 'The ground looks easier.'

It all looked much of a muchness to me. One swamp seemed pretty much the same as another. They'd all feel as cold and sludgy when I traipsed through them.

But he was right. When we set off again the ground did get easier. George seemed to have a real knack for finding the best way through. He guided us around the swamps and kept to the bottom of the ridges, finding little creeks we could follow without having to whack our way through the bush. We made good progress and when we stopped for a rest he turned to me and said, 'See. It's elementary.' He was smiling. And I couldn't help smiling myself then.

A couple of hours later, as we were rounding the edge of a small lake, George said he'd spotted a gap in the trees over to our right. I couldn't see it properly myself, but he insisted it was there so we cut into the bush towards where he said it was. As we got closer I could make out a break in the tops of the taller poplars and white pines, and the trees around us began to thin out. A few feet further on we came to a path. And a foot and a half further, another path.

They were running along beside each other, with bushes and saplings growing in the gap between them. It took us a few seconds to figure it out. They weren't two paths.

They were the tracks of an old road. We'd found the road to Bad Vermillion. We'd found the lost highway.

We kids all knew it was somewhere out there, in the bush to the north and west of us, but we didn't know absolutely for certain. You heard stories about it and that was all.

Nobody in Crooked River liked talking about Bad Vermillion, and when they did their voices dropped till they were almost whispers. They said that before the mine came to Crooked River, it was the big town in these parts – compared to Crooked River, anyhow. It was the only other town in these parts, so I guess there wasn't a bunch of competition. They'd found some gold there a few years after Clarence arrived in Crooked River, and it'd grown fast, until it had two hotels and two stores and its own road. Then the gold had run out and because the railroad didn't run close to it, there was no reason for it being there any more. And that was that. It just sort of faded away. And ever since then it was considered pretty unlucky to even mention its name in Crooked River, as if its bad luck might rub off on us somehow, as if people didn't want reminding that things like that could happen to places. 'Ah, Bad Vermillion – our memento mori,' Virgil used to say, which he told me was a fancy way of saying, 'Remember – this could happen to you!'

George had made plans to find it once. He said we should go on an expedition to 'unearth' it, like some old cities in South America he'd read about in his *National*

Geographics. But in the end we didn't bother. It was a-ways off in the bush and after a while he had to give up on the idea.

You can imagine how pleased he was to find the road to it now, though. A big grin spread right across his face and he kept hopping from one side of the road to the other, through the bushes and the saplings.

'I knew it was here,' he said. 'I found it, Eli. I found it.'

He was right. We had been heading north. But I was right too, because we'd gone west as well.

'I knew it was here,' he said.

George looked a bit surprised when I reminded him we were supposed to be trying to find the river and getting back home. Then he started talking like this had been part of his plan all along. 'That's the thing, Eli. We know where the river is now,' he said. 'We know this road goes north so we know the river's over that way. But we'll never be able to reach it and get back today, will we?'

He was right about that too. The sun was beginning to dip down towards the horizon. There was probably only three hours or so of good daylight left.

'The way I see it we can either camp out here in the open in the bush, or push on till we reach Bad Vermillion. There'll probably be places for us to stay there.'

'But no one lives there no more,' I said. 'We don't know what's there.'

'There's got to be *something*,' he said. 'It's got to be better than being stuck in the bush. We can find the river first thing tomorrow. We know where it is now, don't we?'

The way he was eyeing the road in front of him I knew there was no use arguing. And so off we set, along the lost highway, towards Bad Vermillion.

After a mile or two I'd forgotten my doubts about George's plan. There was a sweet spring smell in the air, of fresh leaves and pine needles, and the hum and bustle of everything beginning to wake up from the winter. George was so excited it was kind of catching. He'd got hold of a stick and was prodding the bush on the sides of the road, looking for stuff, and talking in his *National Geographic* voice about us unearthing things. It made me feel curious too, like him, and I hardly noticed my stomach grumbling. It'd been a while since I'd eaten. I pictured a bowl of porridge. In the back of my mind was the thought that Nana and Dad and Virgil would be worrying about me – but I'd be back tomorrow, I thought. It wouldn't be long. I was imagining me walking in through the porch with George beside me and everyone saying, 'You found him, Eli. Would you believe it? Eli's found him.' Nana would give me a bowl of porridge. Virgil would slap me on the back. Dad would smile. It'd be like I'd caught the best fish in the world.

'Just think,' George said. 'If we kept following this road we'd reach the real north.'

He'd put his stick down by this point and we were walking side by side.

'I guess,' I said.

217

'We could walk and walk and eventually there'd be icebergs and frozen seas and the only people would be Eskimos. We could spear seals and live in igloos and find places nobody had ever been before.'

'I guess,' I said again. I wasn't so sure about the icebergs and igloos. The sun was dropping fast and I was already beginning to feel pretty chilly.

'And this time of year it'd be light all through the night. It'd never get dark. We could get dogs and sleds and ride for as long and as far as we wanted and there'd be no one to stop us. We could go all the way to the North Pole if we wanted to.' He made it sound just like Big Rock Candy Mountain: somewhere you could have everything you wanted.

When I looked over at him, I saw George's eyes had gone kind of red and watery and bloodshot. I guess it must have been from the sun. He didn't have a hat to keep the light off them.

'I don't want to live in Crooked River any more, Eli,' he said. 'I don't want to.'

I gave him my baseball cap. He looked at me with his funny red eyes and his white face.

'Thank you, Eli,' he said.

There wasn't any sign saying welcome to Bad Vermillion. And if there had been, it would've said *Population 0*.

At first we didn't even know we'd reached it. We'd passed a few shacks off the edge of the road, and when we went to look at them we found their roofs had fallen through and bushes and grass were growing up through the floorboards. They didn't look too promising.

'These must be the outskirts,' George said. 'There'll be better places in the centre.'

So we went back to the road and carried on following it. We'd only gone a few hundred yards further along when it ended at the shore of a small lake. There were some mouldy old boards piled up in the woods beside it that must've been boats once. George and me both went a-ways along the shore to look for the rest of Bad Vermillion but we didn't find nothing.

'That must've been it back there,' I said.

'All of it?' George said, looking a bit bewildered.

'I reckon so.'

Further back in the bush, behind the shacks we'd looked at first, we discovered a few more of them. One still had its roof on and pieces of glass in its windows. But there were no old hotels or stores or anything like that. Here and there we stumbled on the wrecks of old-fashioned cars and trucks, dark and cratered with rust and so overgrown with moss and grass and bushes that they looked more like weird-shaped plants. Moving around from shack to shack, we kept on finding other stuff too: a set of swings with pines growing up beneath the poles and a seat hanging off one of the branches; a pair of sneakers that a squirrel had filled with pine cones; an old-time radio with a bent aerial and chewed-up wires sticking out the back. George put that aside for keeping.

We settled on the place with a roof to stay in. The door fell off its hinges with the first push we gave it. Inside the air was still and chilly, as if it hadn't quite shook off the winter yet. There was a table and chairs in the middle of the front room; one of the chairs was pulled out from the table like someone had just that second got up from eating. In the corner was a wood stove, and when we opened it a squirrel scampered out from the nest it'd made in there, stopping for a moment in the middle of the room to give us a disapproving stare before heading out the door.

There were two other small rooms at the back, each with an iron bed frame and a half-eaten mattress on it. There were pieces of pine cone scattered everywhere and in one of the mattresses there was a nest made out of the pages of a chewed-up Bible.

'This'll be perfect,' George said.

I wasn't so sure about that. I couldn't shake off the chill of the place. And when I breathed the air in there it felt strange and stale and thick, like it was full of the spores of someone else's leftover and forgotten life. The light from outside came through the dirty windows and settled in ragged patches on the floor. It was fading. It was getting late.

'I'm hungry,' I said.

'I'll go rustle something up,' George said, bounding out the door.

'Where you going?' I shouted after him.

Nature, to the well-trained eye, is a fully stocked larder, he called back.

I checked out a cupboard in the corner and found a few old cans of beans.

*

It was getting near dark when George came back. He was carrying an armload of twigs and roots and leaves.

'There,' he said, dropping them on the floor. 'Dinner is served.'

'I'm not eating them,' I said.

'They're all edible.'

'For bears, I reckon. I found these,' I said, pointing to the beans.

'Suit yourself.'

But instead of eating his roots and twigs George just stood there, shifting from foot to foot, with his hands in his pockets and a sideways smile on his face. I knew he'd found something else then, besides the leaves.

'What you find?' I asked.

'Come and see,' he said. 'Before it gets too dark.'

Near the end of the road, about five hundred yards or so into the bush, was the remains of a wide clearing. On one side of it was a stagnant-looking pool surrounded by piles of gravel and stones, on the other was a long building made of sheets of corrugated iron, and in between you could see the shapes of rusting pieces of machinery half-hidden beneath bushes and saplings. At the very back of the clearing were the collapsed timbers of a head frame and the big iron drum of a hoist.

'It's the *gold mine*,' George announced, as if it were probably still filled with gold.

We walked a little ways around the edge of the clearing, with George pointing out all the old pieces of machinery and guessing what they'd been for. It was like he was already writing up the cards for them for his collection.

When we got to the pool you could see how its waters were streaked a puke-coloured green and orange, like they were sick.

'There's loads of stuff left behind in the building too,' George said. 'The door's open. I tried it.'

When we got up close to it the head frame looked like a tower made of huge matchsticks that someone had pushed over. The hoist lay just beside it like a giant iron log. And right at the base of the frame you could see the black circle of the mineshaft through the tufts of grass and fireweed that surrounded its edges.

'There's even more stuff further back in the woods,' George said.

Under the trees the shadows had thickened and it was hard to see anything properly. Here and there you could make out other piles of old timber and dark lumps that might have been more pieces of machinery or drums – but you couldn't really tell what anything was in there. Further on there were patches of weak light that could have been other clearings, but the light was fading so fast by then it would have gone by the time you'd have reached them.

'Let's have a look,' George said.

'It's too late,' I said.

'There's still some light.'

'Not enough,' I said, starting to walk back.

George lingered for a few more seconds, and then followed slowly after me as though he didn't really want to.

'You can't keep one eye on the ground in the dark,' I told him.

I didn't get much sleep that night. George went out like a light almost the moment we got into the building and I could hear him breathing peacefully in the corner of the room. But I was cold and the floorboards under me were hard and uncomfortable, and I could hear the squirrels scrabbling around in the other rooms. Lying there awake, I got to thinking about the clearing. There'd been something not quite right about it but I couldn't work out exactly what it was. And then one of the squirrels ran past my feet and I heard an owl hooting outside the window. I knew what it was then. I knew what hadn't seemed quite right.

I hadn't heard a single sound when we walked through it – no crickets, no birds, no frogs, no nothing; only a weird, still quiet that seemed to hang over it. I thought about the sick little pool of water lying out there, in the quiet and the dark, and suddenly felt just about as lonely as could be. I rolled over the floor until I was next to George and snuggled up beside him. Then I listened to his breathing until I fell asleep.

I was woken up by the sound of George pacing noisily about the room. The first light of day was coming in through the windows and when I stretched my arm out I could feel where the floorboards were still warm from where he'd slept on them.

'You ready?' he said. He must have been waiting for me to open my eyes.

'Ready for what?'

'For some exploring. There's loads of stuff past where we stopped yesterday.'

'But we've got to get home,' I said. I was thinking of everyone in the kitchen at number one O'Callaghan Street, looking at maps and worrying. I wished I could be walking in there already.

'There's lots of time for getting home,' George said impatiently. 'We've got this far already – it'd be stupid not to look around and see what's here. We won't be long.'

My whole body was stiff and sore from sleeping on the boards. My stomach was rumbling. I'd had enough of exploring. 'I don't want to be here no more, George. I don't like it. I want to go back.'

George McKenzie could see they'd reached a difficult juncture in their journey and impressed on Mr O'Callaghan the importance of pushing forward with their expedition. To have come this far . . .

'I mean it, George. I don't care about that *National Geographic* shit. It's dumb. It's got shit-all to do with us being stuck out here. I want to go back.'

For a second George looked at me like I'd just punched him in the stomach and I was sorry I'd said all that.

'They'll all be worrying. They've been searching for you for days, George – Virgil and Dad and everybody.'

'Everybody?'

And then he didn't say nothing. His face had gone all loose and scared and blank, the same as when he'd first come out of the underground place. His eyelids blinked fast. And then his expression settled back to normal again and turned hard and determined. His lips were pushed together. When they opened he said:

George McKenzie decided to pursue his course north – alone if need be. There was much to be discovered. The terrain ahead of him had hardly been touched by human feet before, not for many years. It was an almost new land. Nobody knew what was out there.

I walked with George as far as the edge of the clearing. When we got there it was the same as the day before, just as still and quiet and forsaken. The sun was coming up over the tops of the trees and lit up the lonely pool with its sick waters and the rusty shapes of the old machines and the timbers of the fallen tower. You couldn't hear nothing, not a single bird or insect or frog. It was like the world at the very beginning, I thought. Before anything had been made to live in it. Before any creature had tried making it its home.

We stopped and stood there for a bit.

'I don't want to go no further,' I told George. 'I'll wait for you on the road.'

'That's OK, Eli,' George said.

'You won't be long?'

'No,' he said. 'I'll just have a look and then I'll come right back.'

And then he was walking around the edge of the clearing. I watched him go past the pool and the machines, his head moving from side to side, still looking, still curious, still trying to find things, his skin paler than the pale morning light, his lips turned up on one side, smiling his sideways smile. When he reached the other side of the clearing he stopped for a moment by the edge of the treeline. He turned around and looked back at me and his face was like a moth's wing against the green shadows of the woods. And then he was off again, flitting between the trunks and branches. Sometimes I could see him and sometimes I couldn't.

And then I couldn't any more. He was gone.

I couldn't tell how much time went by before I finally went back to the clearing. I sat on a fallen tree trunk by the road for what felt like hours and hours but there was no way of telling how many. I waited until I couldn't any longer and then walked back to look. The sun was high above the clearing but apart from that nothing had changed.

'George,' I shouted. My voice seemed to get swallowed up the moment it came out of my mouth. It was like a drip of water falling onto dry dirt. It barely carried to the other side. There was no answer.

'George.'

It was no use. I'd have to look for him.

When I reached the other side and came to the treeline I began looking for signs. At first there was nothing, but after walking through the trees for a bit I picked up a few footprints in some muddy ground. They led off to the left, towards where I'd thought I'd seen those other clearings the day before.

Sure enough, after a few hundred yards I came to a

second clearing. It was smaller than the first and more overgrown. The bushes and saplings were higher. Some were close to being full trees. I reckoned it must've been abandoned before the other one. It was hard work making my way across it – I had to inch my way bit by bit, pushing through the bushes and saplings and trying to keep my eye on the ground. Here and there I'd manage to pick up signs of George's trail, like footprints and snapped twigs – in one place I even found a little piece of his shirt he'd torn off and tied to a branch as a marker, to help him find his way back – but about halfway across they ran out. I stopped and went back a-ways and made a wide circle through the clearing, trying to pick it up again, but all I found were the remains of some old timber and machinery. And it was a good thing I was watching the ground because just beyond them, tucked away behind a fringe of grass and fireweed, was an old mineshaft. When I'd pushed through the grass and fireweed I'd found it right there below my feet, staring back up at me like a big black eye. I started making my way round it real slow and careful and it was then I picked up George's trail again. There was a set of his footprints near the edge. And then there was nothing.

I can't tell you how many times I walked around the clearing after that. I must've circled it a hundred times, until there wasn't a piece of it I hadn't walked over. And every time it was the same. The trail went one way and then stopped. There was nothing past it, nothing leading out of the clearing. I couldn't find nothing. I went back to the mineshaft and stood at its edge. I stared down at it and it just kept staring back at me. You couldn't see anything down there.

'George,' I shouted.

Nothing.

I picked up a rock and threw it. I heard it clatter against the sides and fall into water. It was a long way down. The sides were steep and sheer.

'George,' I shouted.

I sat down and kept staring into the eye of the shaft, but it never blinked. When I looked up I saw everywhere else had gone dark too.

It was night.

The road seemed to last forever. I was running and running but every time I stopped for breath it was like I'd not gotten anywhere. The branches crowded over my head and reached out to touch my arms and legs. There was no moon or stars and sometimes I'd lose the track and find myself in the woods and spin around crazily till eventually I wound up on it again. But then I must've lost the track one last time and couldn't find my way back onto it. I spun around and around and then just started running as fast as I could through the woods.

The blow-down and the rocks kept tripping me up and the branches scraped my face and arms all over. There was a wet feeling on my skin and I couldn't tell whether it was just sweat or if it was blood from the scrapes – it was too dark to see a thing. And the woods were loud. It was OK when I was running – I couldn't hear nothing but the twigs snapping under my feet and the branches whooshing past my ears and slapping into my face – but the moment I stopped, even for a second, I could hear it: the howling and the hooting and the screeching; the lumbering, crashing noises of invisible animals moving through the bush; and worst of all, the low whispering sounds that seemed to come from all around me – sounds of things I couldn't see and didn't know. I kept running and running to stop myself hearing them, but then my legs wouldn't run no more, so I lay down in a bed of damp moss and curled myself up in a ball and put my hands on my ears to keep them out.

But it wasn't no use.

I couldn't tell where I was or what was around me. There were things beside me, but it was so dark I could only sense they were there – trees and boulders whose shapes I couldn't see but only feel, somehow. It didn't matter whether I closed my eyes. Sometimes I couldn't tell if they were closed or not. And all the time, coming through my fingers into my ears were the whispering sounds.

Sometimes the shapes felt like people and the whispering became their voices. At one point I thought I heard Mr McKenzie and he was saying, 'See. See. This is the end of the world. Didn't you notice, Eli? Didn't you believe me?' And then he was gone and the Earl was there instead. 'This is my Bermuda Triangle,' he was saying. 'This is it. This is it. This is it.' Then he was gone too and George was there.

'Where are you, Eli?' he asked. 'Why aren't you coming with me?'

'George,' I croaked, and my own voice had become as small and weak as a no-see-um. 'I waited, George. I tried following but I lost your trail. I couldn't find it anywhere. Where'd you go?'

'I'm heading north, Eli, to where the icebergs and stuff are. There's a lot to explore there. But I can't see it yet. I've not reached there yet.'

'Where are you, George? I can't see you.'

'I don't know where I am, Eli. It's too dark to see here. I can't see anything here.'

'We've got to get back,' I said. 'We've got to find the Crooked River and get back.'

But he didn't say nothing then. And then the voices got all mixed up into one voice.

'Eli,' it kept whispering. 'Eli. Eli.'

'Eli, Eli,' said the voice, and this time it was just like Virgil's and it was coming from close above me. There were orange and red blotches in the dark in front of me, dancing and jumping about, then a thin sliver of bright light growing wider and brighter. It grew right into daylight. The trees and boulders were there beside me and Virgil's face was peering down at me.

'Thank Christ,' he said. 'It's OK, Eli. It's OK. We've found you. We've found you, thank Christ.'

The kitchen was full of the smell of porridge. There was a big pot of it bubbling on the stove and Nana kept going back and forth, filling up my bowl. Then she would wait behind me while I ate, resting her hand on my shoulder like she was making sure I was really there. It was the warmest, most delicious porridge I'd ever tasted. Nana had put raisins in it and they were hot and sweet. I ate three bowls.

Virgil was sitting at one end of the table and Dad was sitting at the other. They watched me eat – saying nothing at first – looking closely at each spoonful I put in my mouth like they'd never seen anyone eat porridge before. After the second bowl they began telling me what'd happened.

It was Billy who told on me. He must've run right back home after I hit him with the oar and blabbed everything to Buddy. Then Buddy had come over and told Virgil. 'I'm not bothered about the boat,' he'd said. 'I just reckoned you'd want to know. I wouldn't want my kid messing about on that river on his own.' Virgil and Dad set off to find me straight away. They took a canoe and paddled downriver, searching the banks for the rowboat, until at last they found it – right where I'd left it in the reeds and bulrushes. They'd picked up my trail in the mud of the bank and followed it over an outcrop of rock and into the woods. It was there things started getting a little odd, they said.

There were traces of my footprints in the moss and pine needles – they were already pretty faint, only just enough to follow – but overtop of them were a set of bigger, fresher ones. They couldn't figure it out. They didn't know of anyone who came out to this part of the bush – no prospectors or hunters or fishermen – and they couldn't think of anybody who'd have gone out to look for me apart from themselves. And while they were scratching their heads about that, they'd come across what looked like the remains of a clearing. It was real strange, they said. They found an old bear trap under some blueberry bushes and a big mound of earth hidden beneath a pile of blow-down. And then it'd got a whole bunch stranger.

It was Virgil who found the door. He spotted it beside a rock – a set of bare boards in the dirt. When he opened it all he could see to begin with was the top of some steps leading down into a big dark hole. And then, as his eyes adjusted, he made out a face staring up at him and a smaller darker hole.

'You better watch where you're pointing that rifle, Joe,' Virgil said.

'Where've you taken him?' Mr McKenzie hissed.

'I'm not having any conversation with a gun in my face,' Virgil said. 'You put that down and we can talk.'

'Where've you taken him?'

'Taken who?'

'You know damn well who.'

'You better settle yourself down some, Joe. Why don't you come out of there? We're here to find Eli and we'd sure be obliged if you could help us out.'

'*Eli?*'

'That's what I said.'

As Mr McKenzie was coming up the steps, Dad circled behind the door and hit him on the head with a log. He didn't come to till they were back in the boat, they said. And when he did he wasn't any help at all. He just kept babbling on about how they'd stolen George and how they'd all be sorry soon, every damn one of them. He was still saying it when they dropped him off at the police station and headed back down the river.

But the strangest thing of all, Virgil said, was when he took a peek in that hole. He only looked for a second, and there wasn't much light to see by, but he swore there was enough stuff cached down there to live on for years.

I was lucky I'd stayed put so close to the river, Dad and Virgil told me. By the time they'd got to searching for me again the light was getting bad and they couldn't pick up my trail. They'd asked Mr McKenzie where I was about a hundred times, and none too gently neither, but he'd said nothing except how they'd stolen George and how they'd all be sorry before too long. And so they'd combed the bush around the clearing and where they'd found the rowboat until it was dark and then camped out there for the night, meaning to start again at first light. They were expecting help then too, because the police suspected Mr McKenzie had kidnapped George and they were going to send search parties to look in the area around the clearing and off to the north and west of it – up towards Bad Vermillion. But in the end they didn't need any extra help – almost as soon as they'd set off the next morning they'd found me, no more than five hundred yards or so from the boat. They couldn't believe they'd not found me the afternoon before, they said. They both could've sworn they'd covered that very piece of ground.

'Now there's one thing we've got to ask you, Eli,' Virgil said. Dad was nodding his head at the other end of the table. Nana was standing behind me waiting for me to finish my next bowl. Suddenly the porridge didn't feel so good in my stomach.

'We've got to ask you why you took Mr Bryce's boat, Eli. And why you took it all that way down the river.'

'I was looking for George,' I said.

'We kind of guessed that. Nobody's mad with you for trying to find him, Eli, but you know you shouldn't have gone looking for him on your own like that, don't you? Not without telling anyone.'

'I know that,' I said. And that's all I said. There was so much else I should have told them – about George and Bad Vermillion and the mineshaft – but I couldn't. I just couldn't. Even thinking about it all was too much: it was too big a thought for my head, and the words were too big for my tongue.

'Oh . . . and one other thing, Eli. Why did you decide to go in that direction? What made you pick it?'

I said nothing. I couldn't say nothing.

'He must've seen Joe,' Dad said. 'That's it. You saw Joe go that way and you followed him, didn't you, Eli?'

'But the footprints . . .' Virgil started to say.

I left him there. That's all I could think. I left George there alone.

'I think that's enough for now,' Nana said. 'Come with

me, Eli. Why don't you have a lie-down in the living room?'

'I couldn't find him,' I said. My face had gone all wet and I was blubbering. 'I couldn't find him.'

'That's OK, Eli,' Nana said, putting her arm around me. 'You tried. There was nothing more you could do.'

'I waited for him but he didn't come back.'

Nana put me to bed on the couch in the living room, where she could keep an eye on me, and for a long time I just stared at the wall. It's OK, Eli, she kept saying. You're home now.

I stared at the Helsinki picture and the sky was just as blue and full of light as it ever was. And if I looked hard enough it was like I could see George, walking and walking towards the north, towards that same sky – that sky that would never darken and never change, not ever.

Minnow Fishing

The light from the moon didn't last too long. Pretty soon it'd danced and glistened its way off into the night and I was sitting there in the dark, beneath the boughs of the big red pine. I figured it wasn't any use me looking for Bobby if I couldn't see nothing, so I decided to stop and wait till I could see the X Virgil had made on the rock across the river before setting off again.

Virgil never stopped looking for Clarence. Whenever we were out together, fishing or hunting or anything, there was always a piece of him I could tell was keeping one eye out for some sign he'd missed, some clue, some X he'd not thought to mark. And I wondered why that was – why people never stop looking? And do they look back at us, the people who are lost? Are they sad we're gone? Are they looking for us too? Are they waiting to be found? Or do they just want to be left alone?

As soon as the X was visible I got up on my feet. I wasn't really sure what direction to take next but there was this feeling I had that maybe I'd missed something, that there was something I hadn't thought of, so I decided to follow the river down to where it joined the lake and go back along the shoreline. And as I walked I got to thinking about minnow fishing.

If I was a minnow and I was worried about slubes then what would I do? Of course. It was exactly the same as I'd told Bobby: I'd look for cover. So what would seem like the best cover in these parts? There was the woods. That was the obvious choice. Plenty of trees and rocks and stuff to hide behind. But when you really put your mind to it, it's not that easy to hide properly in the woods. Any half-decent slube knows to hunt in the weeds – they're cover for him as much as for the minnows. He just stays still and quiet, and nine times out of ten what he's hunting for comes to him. And the woods would seem just the same. You wouldn't be able to see what was coming for you, and one snapped twig or noisy branch would give you away if it was close. No, what you'd want was a place with a bit of open water around it, to keep an eye on – a reef or something like that. And what looked most like a reef about here? By the time I'd thought it all through I'd gone a-ways down the shoreline and the answer was pretty much staring me in the face: Clarence's castle.

The water around it had dropped to the ground almost – there was only a foot or so left – and it looked almost the same as it did in the photo Jim had taken, except for the trickles of water coming out the windows and the weeds hanging from the sills. With a clear view I reckoned it looked a *bit* like a big barn with a grain tower, but it didn't look *exactly* like that – it didn't look like any building I'd ever seen before. And it was green too, from the slime on the wood.

It was easy enough to walk out to it now, across the exposed mud and shrivelling weeds, and I hadn't gone more than a few feet when I picked up Bobby's tracks. They went down about ten inches into the mud and I couldn't believe I'd missed them the night before. They got shallower and fainter closer to the castle and I figured that must've been because there'd still been water there when Bobby walked out to it. He must've had to swim the last bit because they disappeared altogether before reaching the door.

Bobby must've been a real brave kid. Or a real scared kid. That's what I thought when I stood in front of the door. I didn't want to go in there. It was the last place in the world I wanted to go. I was remembering when the phantom shad had dragged me here before and Clarence and George had beckoned me in. I was remembering dreaming about it, with Dad up above me in the window of the tower, speaking in bubbles. For a long time my feet wouldn't move. This is where all the lost things are, I was thinking. This is where they all live and if I go inside I'll have to live with them for ever.

'Eli?'

It was Bobby's voice. It was coming from up above me, from the tower.

'Eli? Is that you, Eli?' It was hardly more than a whisper.

'Yes. It's me,' I said.

I went inside.

*

Bobby was curled up in the top room of the tower. He was covered from head to toe in mud and slime and was shivering so much he could hardly talk. There were bites all over his face and neck.

'Those bugs sure got you good,' I said.

'Mum says I've got delicate skin.'

'I reckon all those bites should toughen it up.'

'I was hiding.'

'I know you were.'

'Am I in trouble?'

'No,' I said. 'You're not in any trouble. Your mum's worried about you, is all.'

'How'd you find me?'

'It was like minnow fishing,' I told him.

The room was almost empty, like the other rooms below. There was only the silt and slime covering the floor. It was almost empty – except for one chair in the corner opposite where Bobby was. It was turned to face the window that looked out onto where the lake had been and where the river was flowing again now, between its old banks. I hadn't paid much notice to it when I first came in, but as Bobby was getting to his feet I went over there. I'm not sure why I did that, but it was like I had to, somehow – like something was leading me in that direction whether I wanted to go there or not. From behind I could see the remains of what seemed like an old blanket or something, torn and full of holes, hanging off the edge of the seat. It was a faded grey colour. There were a couple of rocks on the floor below it. I went around to the front of the chair to get a better look.

'Eli?' Bobby said from the other side of the room.

I didn't know how long I'd been staring at Clarence when Bobby called – whether it was for seconds or minutes; it was as if, while I stared, seconds and minutes didn't matter any more.

I turned my attention back to Bobby. 'I think we better make tracks now, Bobby,' I said. 'Your mum's real worried about you.' I bundled him down the stairs pretty quick.

As we came out the door Bobby asked, 'Is this where your grandfather lived?'

'No,' I said. 'Not really. Only for a bit. He lived at number one O'Callaghan Street. That's where he lived.'

Bobby and me followed the shore for a while, looking out at the new forest of dead trees that'd grown out of the lake. The river was clear in sight now, meandering its way between them. There were rocks and stumps and other things – things you couldn't tell what they were – strewn across the lake's muddy bed. The sun was creeping over the trees and shining down on them, and in the light they didn't seem so bad.

After a while we cut into the woods and followed Franklin's Trail the rest of the way back to the Poplars. As we were walking Bobby said, 'We can't stay at the Poplars any more, me and Mum.'

'That's what I heard,' I said.

'Billy wants me to live with him but I don't want to.'

'I know.'

'That's why I was hiding.'

'I know.'

'Mum doesn't know where else we can go.'

'I've been thinking about that,' I said. 'I've got a plan about it.'

'What plan?'

'I've got a place, Bobby. Number one O'Callaghan Street. It's where Clarence lived. Buddy says it's not fit to live in but I reckon with a bit of work it'd be fine.'

'And can me and Mum live there?'

'I'd like you both to live there,' I said. 'If you want to.'

Under the Helsinki Sky

It wasn't as hard as I thought – fixing up number one O'Callaghan Street. Sarah and Bobby gave me a hand. While I put in the new boards in the porch Bobby held the nails for me and Sarah started painting the walls, wearing her red duck hat. Buddy seemed pretty pleased with the whole thing. He stopped mentioning that I might want to pull the place down; instead he spent a lot of time sitting out in his garden, coming over to the fence every half-hour or so to give me advice. 'You might want to think about using white paint for those window frames,' he might say; or, 'Why not plant some roses along the fence here, Eli? They'd go well with the lilies on this side.' He was happy to have Bobby there too, you could tell. He bought him a bunch of candy, just like he was King of Big Rock Candy Mountain again.

Billy, meantime, had gone up north for the summer to fly for an outfitters' near Lake St Joseph. He'd kind of lost interest in Bobby when he found out he got the job – which was just like Billy: he always preferred new things.

I fixed up the inside as well as the outside. A lot of stuff I hadn't touched or moved for years, but now I went through it all and made a big pile out in the garden. I was planning to take it to Gracie and Mr Haney at the museum to see if they thought any of it was historical and worth keeping. I kept all of Virgil's books, though, and his and Dad's record collection – even though I didn't have anything to play them on. Dad and Virgil's record player had definitely become historical, meaning it didn't work no more.

And I kept the Helsinki picture too. I took it off the wall and brought it down into the basement. I'd put Clarence safely in his trunk by then, together with his other things. I figured there wasn't any need to let Officer Red or anybody else know about him. Let him lie still now, I thought. Let him lie still and quiet. There were no more circles he needed to spin in, no more endlessly looping rivers. I put the Helsinki picture on top of him – so he'd always have something to look at, so the sky above him would always be blue and full of light – and then closed the trunk.

There was just one more thing I needed to do.

Buddy let me use his truck to take the pile of stuff to the museum, and on my way I stopped at the police station. Officer Red was outside polishing his car. It gets a lot of dust on it when he's out driving about looking for crimes.

'Hey there, Eli,' he said. 'And to what do I owe the pleasure . . . ? What'll it be you're wanting?'

'I guess I just wanted a word,' I said.

Afterwards I went straight on to the museum. I parked

up beside Clarence's canoe, and when I got out I found Mr Haney wobbling about on a ladder propped by the front door.

'I don't know what's with this sign,' he said. 'It won't stay put for love nor money.'

IAL, it said. *01*.

'What've you got in the truck there, Eli?'

'It's from my house,' I said. 'I'm fixing it up. I thought you might want some of the stuff for the museum.'

'That's very thoughtful of you, Eli,' Mr Haney said, climbing down from the ladder.

'Is Gracie in?' I asked him.

Mr Haney came with me to the door. When he opened it, I could see Gracie was in her office from the big clouds of smoke behind the glass.

'Eli has brought us some potential artefacts for the museum,' Mr Haney said. 'I think they could prove a real treasure trove.'

'You been clearing the junk out of your basement then, Eli?' Gracie asked.

'Kind of,' I said.

I shuffled my way closer to her. It seemed like a long way. I opened my mouth to speak but the first two times nothing came out.

'Are you OK, Eli?' Gracie asked.

I opened my mouth a third time.

'I got something I got to tell you,' I said.

Everything All at Once

From the windows of the plane you could see everywhere spread out below. There was Eye Lake, muddy brown and flecked silver with pools and puddles; and Red Rock Lake, glinting and glistening and full of water. You could see the line of Main Street and O'Callaghan Street and the whole town, stained a faint red by the dust. And you could see the Crooked River – meandering its way through them, joining them up like dots on a zigzagging puzzle. And surrounding everything, stretching away as far as you could see in every direction, the ragged pattern of forests and creeks and lakes, like a huge piece of torn green cloth floating on blue.

I'd never seen it from above like this. I'd never been in a plane before. I liked the way you didn't have to look backwards or forwards to look at it. From up here you could see everything all at once.

The plane's engines hummed and puttered. We rose up and up and then began to dip down. We weren't going far. Only as far as Bad Vermillion.

'Are you sure you'll be able to remember this place?' Officer Red hollered from the other end of the plane.

'I'll remember it,' I said.

Gracie was sitting on the seat opposite mine. She was staring out the window behind my head. Her eyes were black like the owl's. She hadn't said a word to me since the museum the day before. As the plane dipped further down I said, 'I'm sorry, Gracie.'

She didn't say nothing.

'I'm sorry,' I said.

'I don't want to talk about this, Eli,' she suddenly said, still staring out the window behind my head. 'I don't want to talk about it, not now.'

The plane started to bank and through the window I could see the corner of Bad Vermillion Lake coming into view.

'I just want to find him,' Gracie said. 'And then it'll be over.'

Acknowledgements

This book was nurtured and written in many different houses and homes. I would like to offer my thanks and gratitude to all those who provided them: to Beatrice von Rezzori and everyone at the Santa Maddalena Foundation; to the Translators' House Wales and Halma Network for residencies in Minsk and Rhodes; to Igor and Volja at the Logvinov Publishing House in Minsk; and to the International Writers' and Translators' Centre of Rhodes. I would also like to thank Jordi Punti, for the conversations at Santa Maddalena during which this novel first came to life for me; and Sam Humphreys and Veronique Baxter for their help and encouragement. And finally Lisa Solomon, for her generosity and support and so much more. Diolch o galon.

picador.com

blog
videos
interviews
extracts